HUNTING SEASON

It was the height of the London Season—when society mingled and marriages were made.

For the Marquis of Rayleigh, it was a time to tame Jane Fitzmaurice, who had become his ward as an unspoiled child and now had grown to be an outrageously head-strong young woman.

For young Lord Audley, it was a season to snare Lady Jane, the only female in England who didn't swoon at the idea of him as a suitor.

For David Chance, Jane's childhood companion, it was the long-dreaded moment to face being torn from her by all the forces of wealth and privilege.

And for Jane, it was a season to be herself and have what she wanted. . . .

A LONDON SEASON

Recommended Regency Romances from SIGNET

A
London Season

by
Joan Wolf

A SIGNET BOOK
NEW AMERICAN LIBRARY
TIMES MIRROR

PUBLISHER'S NOTE

This novel is a work of fiction. Names, characters, places, and incidents are either the product of the author's imagination or are used fictitiously, and any resemblance to actual persons, living or dead, events, or locales is entirely coincidental.

Copyright © 1980 by Joan Wolf

SIGNET TRADEMARK REG. U.S. PAT. OFF. AND FOREIGN COUNTRIES REGISTERED TRADEMARK—MARCA REGISTRADA HECHO EN CHICAGO, U.S.A.

SIGNET, SIGNET CLASSICS, MENTOR, PLUME, MERIDIAN AND NAL BOOKS are published by The New American Library, Inc., 1633 Broadway, New York, New York 10019

First Printing, January, 1981

1 2 3 4 5 6 7 8 9

PRINTED IN THE UNITED STATES OF AMERICA

Chapter I

My child is yet a stranger in the world. . . .
—William Shakespeare

Lady Jane Fitzmaurice was six years old when her parents were killed.

She came riding home to Loughmore Castle late in the afternoon, muddy and windblown as she always was after a day spent cantering her pony over the green hills of Tipperary. There was no sign on that lovely Irish spring day that anything unpleasant could possibly threaten her secure young life. She left her pony at the stables and walked up to the great stone house, home of the Earls of Loughmore for generations. She knew her parents had gone boating on Lough Derg, but their absence made little impression on her. She rarely saw them even when they were at home.

She had her dinner in the nursery with Miss Kilkelly as usual. Then she looked through a book on horses that had been given to her for her last birthday, and allowed Miss Kilkelly to wash her and put her to bed.

The news was brought to the castle an hour after Jane was asleep. A squall had come up suddenly on Lough Derg and the small boat

1

containing the Earl, the Countess, and their two friends had capsized. None of the party could swim. There were no survivors.

The news was broken to Jane by the local rector. He sat before the Kilkenny marble fireplace in the drawing room and Jane stood before him. She was dressed, as always, in riding clothes and the rector hesitated, searching for the right words to use to the small, self-possessed child in front of him.

Jane Fitzmaurice was not a pretty child, but there was something unusual in the high cheekbones and square jaw that promised more than prettiness as she grew older. Her hair was black and hung straight as rain down her back, tied at her nape by an old velvet ribbon. Her eyes, the blue-green of the sea on sunny days, looked straight at Reverend Linley.

The rector spoke gently. "Jane, I'm afraid I have bad news for you. Your mother and father had an accident with the boat...."

He hesitated. "Yes?" Jane said in her clear, child's voice.

"They were drowned, Jane," he said. "I am so sorry, my dear."

"Drowned?" A frown appeared between Jane's brows. "Do you mean they are dead, Reverend Linley?"

"Yes." Helplessly the rector looked at the small, slim figure in front of him. Himself the father of three, his impulse was to reach out and hug her. But the erect, solitary child who was watching him with such steady eyes did not appear to be at all in need of comfort.

There was a long silence, then Jane said slowly, "Will I be able to stay at Loughmore Castle?"

The rector blew his nose. "The estate is entailed, Jane," he said after he had put his handkerchief back in his pocket. "Do you know what that means?"

"It means it cannot come to me because I am a girl. Who will it go to, rector?" For the first time there was a tremor in the self-possessed voice. "Will I be able to stay here?"

The rector was tempted to say something soothing, but found it impossible to lie to those direct blue-green eyes. "I don't know, Jane," he said honestly. "We shall have to wait and see."

Jane was the only child of James Fitzmaurice, Earl of Loughmore, and his wife Helen. Her sex had been a grevious disappointment to her parents, a disappointment that became more bitter as the years went by and no more children appeared. When James was drowned, Loughmore Castle passed into the hands of his second cousin, Henry Fitzmaurice, who became the fifth Earl. Jane passed into the guardianship of her maternal uncle, Edward Stanton, Marquis of Rayleigh. The Marquis was only twenty-six years of age, but as Lady Loughmore's only brother he was Jane's nearest surviving relative and so had been designated her guardian in her father's will.

Her parents' death made no great impression

on Jane, as she had hardly ever seen them, but
leaving Loughmore was anguish. Her parents had
ignored her and there were no other children
about with whom she could play, but she had had
her pony and the grooms in the stable who had
taught her to ride when she was two. It was not a
normal childhood, but it was the only sort of life
Jane had ever known. In the way of children, she
had accepted it as ordinary. She had not been unhappy.

Now she was to leave Loughmore. Leave Ire-
land, in fact, and cross the sea to a strange land
she had never seen, to live with an uncle she had
never met. For the first time in her young life she
was afraid.

But even at six years of age, Jane Fitzmaurice
had too much pride to allow anyone to suspect her
feelings. The only time she let down was when
she realized she would have to leave her pony behind. She cried then, lying in the darkness of her
bed at night. She had not cried about her parents.

The only comforting news Jane had heard since
the rector told her of the death of her parents was
the fact that her Uncle Edward's house was near
Newmarket and that it was a stud. There would
be horses, Jane told herself over and over. If there
were horses it could not be so bad.

She was to travel to England with her nurse,
Miss Kilkelly, and her Uncle Edward's secretary,
who had been dispatched from Heathfield, the
Marquis's estate, to make sure she arrived safely.

Packing Jane's clothes and belongings did not take very long. She was not a child who was interested in pretty dresses, and her mother, who thought her plain, had rarely troubled about what she had to wear. Most of her clothes were riding things.

They traveled from Loughmore to Wexford and from Wexford across St. George's Channel to Wales. The crossing was calm and Jane had remained on deck the whole time, silent and reserved as she had been since Mr. Hightower, her uncle's secretary, had arrived at Loughmore. He was a man of about fifty and unused to children, but he had tried to be kind to her. It worried him that she was so quiet. He had expected her to be full of questions about her new home, but beyond asking him how many horses there were at Heathfield she had said nothing. Her cousin, the new Earl, had tried to be kind as well, and had met with the same polite lack of response.

The trip across England seemed interminable to Jane. They arrived in Newmarket early in the evening six days after they had set out from Wales. Jane was dazed from tiredness and with difficulty took in the great stone house with its high chimneys and many windows glowing in the light of the setting sun.

She stumbled a little as she stepped out of the carriage, but resolutely shook off Miss Kilkelly's helping hand. She straightened her back and walked directly up the front steps to the dark-haired young man who was waiting for her. The Marquis of Rayleigh was dressed in immaculate evening attire, the whiteness of his snowy shirt and cravat in marked contrast to Jane's wrinkled and travel-stained coat and dress. "Are you my Uncle Edward?" Jane asked, ever direct.

"Yes." The young man's smile was a trifle rueful as he surveyed the untidy, resolute figure before him.

She nodded and walked past him into the beautiful marble hall. Her eyes went immediately to the paintings that decorated its walls. Most of them were by George Stubbs; they were all of horses.

"Oh," said Jane, and a sparkle began to glow in her strangely light eyes.

Her uncle came up behind her and said cheerfully, "I don't quite know what I'm to do with you, Jane. I have had no experience with children, I'm afraid. But I did buy two ponies for you to ride. Perhaps you'd care to look at them in the morning?"

Jane turned around and looked at him, the glow in her eyes more pronounced. "Ponies, for me?" she said carefully. "Are they mine?"

"Certainly," said Edward Stanton. "They are yours."

She went upstairs to the nursery with Miss Kilkelly shortly after that, leaving her uncle to invite his secretary to share a glass of brandy with him. After he dismissed Mr. Hightower the Marquis sat on for another hour while he consumed another brandy on his own. On the whole he was relieved by his secretary's report.

Edward Stanton was only twenty-six years of age and had been deeply dismayed to hear he was to become the guardian of a six-year-old child. It was a responsibility he most definitely did not want, but, as his solicitor had made perfectly clear, he was Jane's only close relative. "The child must live somewhere, my lord," was how Mr. Abercrombie had phrased it. "If not with you, then where?"

So the Marquis had given instructions for the nursery at Heathfield to be opened up and, being a Stanton, he had immediately made sure his niece would have horses to ride. Beyond that, he thought helplessly, he would have to rely on the child's nurse.

Jane was not at all what he had expected. When he had looked into her eyes, the same aquamarine color as her father's, he remembered dimly, he had had the feeling he was looking at a person, not merely an anonymous child. She did not look at all helpless. And from what Hightower had told him, she seemed very well able to take care of herself. If he just left her to her own devices, his lordship thought hopefully, perhaps she would manage very well without him.

Jane awoke early the next morning to find the sun streaming in the window of a strange room. It took her a minute to realize that this was not yet another inn, but Heathfield itself. Her new home.

She sat up in bed, pushed her hair out of her eyes, and looked curiously about her. The nursery

walls were painted a pale shade of blue that com-
plemented the blue in the tiles around the fireplace. Crisp white curtains hung at the windows
and the wide-planked floor shone with polish. In a
minute Miss Kilkelly came in to lay out Jane's
clothes for the day.

"I'm going riding, Kelly," Jane told her, a hint
of excitement in her voice. "Uncle Edward bought
two ponies for me. He told me to look at them
this morning."

"That's nice, Lady Jane," said Miss Kilkelly
composedly. Without fuss she began to lay out one
of Jane's better riding outfits, no hint on her face
of the relief she felt at that note of enthusiasm in
Jane's clear voice.

After Jane was dressed, she and Miss Kilkelly
went into the next room where a small table was
set up in front of the window. A housemaid came
in with their breakfast, which Jane ate as quickly
as possible, eager to be off to the stables.

By nine o'clock she was walking down the half-
mile gravel drive that led from the house to the
stableyard.

Chapter II

Delight and liberty, the simple creed of Childhood. . . .

—William Wordsworth

David Chance finished his breakfast an hour before Jane that morning and reached the stables
thirty minutes before she did.

"Lady Jane arrived last night, David," Tuft, the
head groom, informed him. "We've had word that
she's going to ride this morning. You'd better
saddle up both ponies and go with her. I expect
she'll enjoy having a child her own age to talk to."

"I'm not her age; I'm seven," David said
through shut teeth and, scowling ferociously, disappeared into the stables.

When the Marquis had bought Jane's ponies
three weeks ago, there had been a moment's consternation about who was to exercise them until
she arrived. All of the grooms were too heavy.
However, it had not taken long for David
Chance's name to come up and once someone had
thought of him the matter was as good as settled.

David lived with his aunt, Mademoiselle
Héloise Dumont, in a small cottage not far from
Heathfield. They were French émigrés, but since

9

David had resided in Newmarket since he was a
year old, he regarded himself as totally English.
They were not well off; Mlle. Dumont gave
French and piano lessons to supplement their income. But they owned the cottage and there was
always enough to put food on the table and
clothes on their backs.

Mlle. Dumont was not greatly liked in the
neighborhood. She considered her social station
superior to that of the people with whom she
came into contact. Her father had been a well-to-
do lawyer, she was fond of telling anyone who
would listen, and were it not for that dreadful
revolution she would be living in luxury in
France, not making do in a poor English cottage.

The local townsfolk privately thought she was
lucky to still have her head. As she was a good
teacher, they sent their daughters to her to learn
French and piano, but otherwise they ignored her.

David was more popular. He was shy, but there
was a gentleness about him that touched the heart
of many a village matron. His parents had died in
France and he was universally pitied for that misfortune as well as for the trial of having to live
with Mlle. Dumont. David's aunt was sharp-
tongued and bitter, and ever since he could walk
the two miles David had been escaping to Heathfield to look at the horses. The beautiful, shining
thoroughbreds bore little resemblance to the ancient cob his aunt kept, and when one of the
grooms had put him up on the glossy chestnut

back of a small mare, he had felt that life could hold no more for him.

The chance to ride Jane's ponies had been heaven. Even at age seven, David was a natural horseman, which is why the grooms at Heathfield had taken such an interest in him. He had light yet firm hands and, what was really unusual in so young a child, infinite patience.

He had loved riding Mindy and Flash and he resented bitterly the fact that they would go to an Irish brat—a girl, too—whom he was sure would not ride them properly. There was little evidence of David's famous good nature as he stood brushing Mindy's coat. He was muttering darkly to himself, braced to dislike on sight the Irish brat who was stealing his horses.

The stables at Heathfield were as impressive in their own right as the house was. There were two long blocks of brick stables facing each other over an immaculate stableyard. Across the far end was a wing which connected the two blocks. The wing contained the office, a large tack room, and an even larger feed room. Behind the stable were a series of paddocks and beyond the paddocks the famous Newmarket Heath.

Jane's eyes shone with appreciation as she took in the rows of stalls with well-groomed horses' heads looking over the half-opened doors. There was room for at least forty horses here, she thought with deep satisfaction.

A man of about fifty-five came up to her, his

eyes very blue in his weatherbeaten face. "Lady Jane?" he said. "I'm Tuft, the head groom. His lordship sent word you'd be wanting to ride this morning."

"Yes." Jane gave him her rare smile. "I should like to look around the stables when I return, Tuft. They look excellent." *Excellent* was Jane's latest favorite word and she used it whenever possible.

"Certainly, Lady Jane," replied the groom. "Be glad to show you around. Here is David now with your ponies."

David had heard her last remark and the corners of his sensitive mouth were curled with scorn. "Excellent," he thought to himself derisively. What did she know about the stables being excellent? He stared at Jane with inimical eyes as Tuft introduced them.

"Lady Jane, this is David Chance. He has been exercising your horses for the last three weeks. I thought perhaps you might like him to show you around."

Jane looked at David, missing completely the hostility in his eyes. She liked what she saw. He was a slim boy about two inches taller than she, but it was his coloring that caught instantly at her attention. He was all brown and gold. His light brown hair had bleached into streaks of blond and his skin was light gold, the color that fair skin turns when exposed to the sun. The eyes that were staring so implacably at her were the color of sherry wine, flecked with gold around the pupil.

Jane made up her mind. "You ride the bay, David," she motioned to the horse he was holding, "and I'll ride this one." Unself-consciously she turned to Tuft, who gave her a leg up into the saddle.

David stared at her for another minute before following suit. She was not quite what he had expected. For one thing, she wore breeches and boots just like a boy, and for another, she looked very much at home as she picked up Mindy's reins and turned her toward the heath.

"Wait a minute, Lady Jane," said Tuft, "and I'll get Thompson to go with you."

"That won't be necessary," Jane said imperiously. "David will show me." She nudged Mindy with her heels and cantered sedately out of the yard; David followed.

They passed the paddocks at the same easy pace, but once they were well out in the open Jane turned to David. "Let's gallop," she said.

By the time they pulled their ponies up by a wooded copse, David had banished every unpleasant thought he had ever had about the "Irish brat." Jane Fitzmaurice could ride!

He turned to her, laughing with pleasure, and she laughed back. Suddenly he leaned over to her, his hand extended. "I'm glad you've come, Jane," he said. She took his hand, vaguely aware that it was some sort of a peace offering. "I'm glad, too," she said. And meant it.

The first morning of Jane's arrival they had

spent three hours out on the heath. Tuft had been very worried; if something happened to Lady Jane he knew he would get the blame for letting her go off with just David. He had been deeply relieved when they rode in, slightly dirty and obviously on very good terms with each other.

"I'll show Jane around the stables," David offered after they had dismounted and she had given a small piece of carrot to each pony.

"Lady Jane, David," Tuft corrected the boy firmly.

Jane stared at the groom. "What David calls me is none of your affair, Tuft," she said haughtily. "Besides, he's my friend."

David looked at her small, flushed face and grinned. "Come on, Jane," he said. "Let's start with Pharaoh."

The next day they rode out again together and this time David had a treat for her. "Do you want to see my secret place, Jane?" he asked, and for the first time she noticed that his eyes turned golden when he was excited.

"Your secret place? Your very own?" she said in hushed tones.

"Yes. No one knows about it but me."

"I'd love to see it," Jane said solemnly, suitably impressed by the honor he was bestowing on her.

"Come on, then," and David moved off toward a thick wood in the distance. They entered the wood by a narrow trail, but soon David veered off among the trees, Flash's hooves making snapping sounds as he trod on fallen branches and old dried leaves.

Jane followed, filled with admiration for his sure sense of direction. As they came out of the woods and into a small clearing, she gasped with surprise.

There was a small lake, hardly more than a pond, fed by a stream that tumbled down a narrow waterfall into a smaller pool and then disappeared among the trees in a swiftly-running river. The water in the pond looked still, reflecting back the brightness of the sky. The only sound to be heard was the splash of water from the falls. "Oh, David," Jane said reverently, as she dismounted from Mindy and walked to the edge of the water which was banked by a stretch of grass. "It's just excellent."

He smiled as he remembered his feelings the last time he had heard that word. Now he was pleased by her praise. "I found it two years ago," he told her. "I come here when I want to be alone."

Jane nodded in perfect comprehension. "Will you let me share it?" she asked humbly.

"Of course," he answered matter-of-factly. "That's why I brought you here."

She smiled at him as if she had been given a fabulous gift, as indeed she had been.

From then on they were Jane-and-David, a twosome, linked together against the outside world. There was never a time when either child had put into words their need of each other; it

was something they understood instinctively. Jane
was temperamental and David was serene. Jane
was the niece of a Marquis and David's aunt gave
French lessons. They were different in so many
ways, but in the most important way of all they
were alike. It was not something that needed to be
said. Simply, for the first time in their lives each
child had someone he loved.

Chapter III

Here's one a friend, and one that knows you well.
  —William Shakespeare

All through that first summer of their friendship, Jane and David ran free. They rode their horses; it was understood, without ever having to be said, that Flash belonged to David. Jane never asked to ride him and very soon he was even referred to by the grooms as "David's pony."

They spent many hours in their secret place and, to Jane's great delight, David taught her how to swim. "My parents drowned," she had told him solemnly, looking at the calm water of their lake.

"You'd better let me teach you to swim," he had answered practically, which seemed to Jane an admirable solution to her unspoken fear. Obviously she couldn't drown if she knew how to swim. Soon she and David were splashing happily in the water, unself-conscious in their underwear, which they dried by stretching themselves full-length on their grassy beach. David kept an old scythe hidden in the woods and by this simple expedient they kept the wild grass cut to a comfortable length.

By the end of the summer David was deeply

17

tanned and even Jane's translucent skin had taken
on a peach-brown color. They were strong and
healthy and, in the way of children, looked for
their pleasant life to continue without interruption.

The first snake in their garden appeared in
early September when Jane's uncle returned from
a race meeting to find that Miss Kilkelly had
asked for an interview with him.

"It's about Lady Jane's education, my lord," she
began diffidently when he had sent for her to attend him in the library.

The Marquis knit his dark brows and stared
thoughtfully at the small, plump, middle-aged
person before him. "Yes, I suppose I must do
something about it," he sighed. "Won't do to let
her run wild completely, I suppose. Still, she looks
marvelously healthy. And she certainly can ride!
Tuft tells me she has the best hands on a horse
he's ever seen." The Marquis's handsome, indo-
lent face looked impressed.

Miss Kilkelly, who did not share the Stanton
passion for horses, was impatient. "There is more
to life than horses, my lord," she said, a trifle
tartly.

The Marquis cocked an eyebrow. "If you say so,
Miss Kilkelly. I hate to pull the reins in on the
child, though. She is obviously enjoying herself
enormously, I remember when I was that
age. . . ." The Marquis sighed nostalgically,
then caught the implacable eye of Miss Kilkelly,
who reminded him uncomfortably of an old nurse

of his own. "Yes, well I suppose we must engage a governess," he said hastily. "I'll see about it, Miss Kilkelly."

"Thank you, my lord," she said approvingly.

The next person to demand an interview with him was Jane herself. She had heard about the governess from Miss Kilkelly and, without waiting to change her riding clothes, had sought her uncle out immediately. He had just come in from a drive to the Rivingdale's, who were spending a few weeks at their Newmarket residence, and she found him in the marble hall, beautifully dressed as usual. "I must speak to you, Uncle Edward," she said in her clear child's voice. "Are you busy at present?"

"Not at all, Jane," he replied courteously. "Come into the library." He held the door for her and watched the small black head march past him, a glint of amusement in his eyes. He had seen little of Jane since she had arrived at Heathfield, but what he had seen of her he liked. She had made herself a favorite in the stables and she didn't seem to expect anything of him. If one had to be saddled with a small girl, he thought as he closed the door behind her, Jane was obviously the best one could hope for.

"Sit down, Jane," he said kindly. Then, when she had complied, "What can I do for you?"

She had been looking with approval at his russet coat and polished top-boots, which satisfied her color-loving eye, but as he spoke her blue-green eyes darkened.

"I don't want a governess," she said firmly.

"I see." He regarded her gravely. "You have to have some form of education, Jane. When your parents named me as your guardian, they trusted me to see to it that you were brought up in a manner befitting your name and your position."

"I know I have to have an education," she said reasonably. "I just don't want a governess. I want to go to Reverend Althorpe's with David."

"Reverend Althorpe?"

"Yes. He's the rector at St. Margaret's. He is going to teach David Latin and mathematics and geography and everything. He will be much more interesting than a governess," Jane said firmly.

"I see," he said again. The prospect of his small niece learning Latin was somewhat daunting. "Girls, you know, my dear Jane, don't usually study the same things boys do."

"Why not?" Jane said uncompromisingly.

"Well, er, their role in life is different, Jane. They must learn music and, ah, sewing, Italian. . . ."

"Italian?" Jane looked astonished. "Why on earth should I want to learn Italian?"

"I don't know," he answered truthfully. "Females always do, though."

"Well, it all sounds to me like a waste of time. Latin sounds a waste, too, but I suppose I must study something. Besides," Jane said, as if that clinched the matter, "David is doing it."

"Yes, but——" the Marquis was beginning.

"And," she went on inexorably, "I can study

French and piano from David's Tante Héloise. I think I should take a lot of lessons. They need the money."

A rueful smile crossed Lord Rayleigh's face. "How old are you, Jane?"

"Seven next month."

He looked at the small, determined face of his niece. "If you are like this at six, God help us all when you are sixteen. All right. You can go to Reverend Althorpe with your precious David. Just don't ask me to conjugate your verbs for you."

She gave him a brilliant smile, which momentarily lit her plain face to beauty. "Thank you, Uncle Edward." She skipped to the door, turning to ask as she reached it, "No more governess?"

"No more governess," he promised, conscious that he had given in to her shamefully. She had not coaxed or charmed him. It was simply that he feared if it came to a real battle of wills between them, Jane's would prove to be the stronger.

So Jane and David became scholars together, meeting every morning in the stable office at Heathfield and riding dutifully to the rectory at St. Margaret's some five miles away.

Mr. Althorpe was a gentle, scholarly man who occasionally took on pupils in order to supplement his income. Both Jane and David learned to read with astonishing rapidity. Mr. Althorpe was very impressed with their evident enthusiasm. He would have been sadly disillusioned to discover that the main reason they were so anxious to learn was so they could read the *Racing Calendar* by themselves.

Jane's French lessons went well, also. David spoke French fluently so Jane, always anxious to keep up with him, attacked it with vigor. Her piano lessons went less successfully. She had no ear for music at all and only played when actually taking the lesson from David's aunt. Much as Mlle. Dumont urged her to practice at home, the great piano in the drawing room at Heathfield remained untouched. Jane had better things to do.

In the good weather the two children would ride out by themselves, exploring every corner of West Suffolk on their ponies. They kept most often to the rolling downs, but they became a familiar sight as well in Newmarket and the local villages.

The heath, of course, fascinated them. The sight of the Marquis's horses and the horses from other studs in the area, their gleaming coats shining in the sun as they were galloped in the early-morning workouts, affected Jane more profoundly than the most beautiful music ever could.

They could often be found on Marren Hill, which was not used by the stables as was nearby Warren Hill. Marren was too steep for a horse to canter up it; it had only a few narrow paths, more ably climbed by humans than by horses. On one side there was an old quarry gouged into the hillside. Jane and David would often climb the hill, leaving their ponies tethered to a tree at the bottom, and picnic among the old beeches that grew on the hillside overlooking the quarry.

They took over a corner of the tack room where they would sit on rainy days pouring over the *Racing Calendar* and the *General Stud Book*. As the years passed and their apprenticeship with Reverend Althorpe lengthened, their reading material broadened considerably. Plutarch's *Lives*, Cook's *Voyages*, Goldsmith's *History of Rome*, Robertson's *History of America*, were all devoured and discussed with enthusiasm.

They were both indifferent Latin scholars. Privately Jane confided to David that since they were never going to have to talk to anybody in Latin, she didn't see any reason in learning it. David agreed. After all, he pointed out, all the great books written in Latin had been translated into English anyway. They were both well acquainted with the translations, cribbing from them mercilessly rather than making the effort to translate on their own.

They persevered with Mr. Althorpe, although they were convinced that they learned more by themselves reading in the tack room. As they grew older, Tuft allowed them to help with the Marquis's thoroughbreds, and by the time Jane was ten and David was eleven they were riding some very expensive horseflesh in training gallops over Newmarket Heath.

Tuft had gotten permission from Lord Rayleigh before he put them up. "Those children have the best hands and seats of anyone in the stable, my lord," he had said frankly.

"Can they hold a thoroughbred, though, Tuft?" the Marquis had asked incredulously.

"Not all of 'em, my lord. At least not yet. But mark my words, David will be able to ride anything in a few years' time."

"And Lady Jane?"

Tuft heaved a heartfelt sigh. "I don't want to be forward, my lord, but it's often I've been sorry Lady Jane was born a girl. She's a little lass, but she can hold her own with at least four horses who'll be running next year."

The Marquis, who saw his niece more frequently at the stable than he did under his own roof, privately agreed. He gave permission for Jane and David to ride his horses, and both children plunged into the demanding routine of a racing stable with an intense enthusiasm that neither falls nor sore muscles could diminish.

Chapter IV

I do but keep the peace. . . .
—William Shakespeare

David lay stretched out on the grassy bank that
bordered their private lake and watched Jane fishing. She was standing on a flat rock a little way
out from the shore, a rod in her hand. Her gaze
was intent upon the quiet water; she looked as if
she were *willing* a fish to bite her line, he thought
in lazy amusement.

He watched her quietly, enjoying the warmth
of the sun on his back. She had grown taller this
past year, he thought. The legs that were revealed
by her shamelessly hitched-up skirt were long and
slim. There was a tug on her line and he sat up as
she pulled in her catch, every motion of her body
suggesting the accomplished poise of an acrobat.

She grasped the fish firmly and waded back to
the shore where she threw herself down beside
David. Next to him she scarcely seemed tanned at
all, but her neck under her tied-back hair was
milk-white compared to the faint gold of her
cheeks. "I wish we could stay here always," she
said intensely. "Just the two of us."

He nodded understandingly. For the past week

they had been embroiled in what David called privately "The Battle of the Sidesaddle."

It had begun when the Marquis had invited a group of friends down for a house party and they had all gone hunting. Jane and David had gone along as well, as they had been doing for the past year.

They had had an excellent run, both children distinguishing themselves by jumping a fence that had a bad, sloping take-off that necessitated jumping from almost a walk. The majority of the field had detoured around it.

It was after dinner that evening that Lady Sarah Hadden had commented with surprise that Jane was still allowed to ride astride. "How old is she now, my lord?" she asked the Marquis innocently.

Lord Rayleigh had to think for a moment. "Twelve," he said finally.

"Twelve! I'm surprised her governess allows it."

The Marquis felt faintly uncomfortable. "I'm afraid she hasn't got a governess, Lady Sarah."

"She hasn't got a governess!" Lady Sarah stared at him in genuine amazement.

"Then who teaches her, my lord?" joined in Mrs. Carsford, who had been listening.

"She goes to the Rectory at St. Margaret's," he said defensively. "The Reverend Mr. Althorpe is a highly respected scholar. I might say that he has the greatest respect for Jane's ability." A well-developed sense of self-preservation prevented him from mentioning she was partnered in her studies by a local boy whom he had engaged to work in his stables for the summer.

"How very odd," Mrs. Carsford murmured, her thin brows raised. "But Sarah is right, you know, my lord. She really should not ride astride at her age."

So the edict had come down from Lord Rayleigh: Lady Jane was to learn to ride sidesaddle. Jane had looked with revulsion on the awkward saddle and had stalked out of the stables and into the house where she found her uncle having breakfast.

"I will not ride that thing," she said fiercely, planting herself directly across the table from him.

"Yes, you will," he said. "All the ladies were horrified to see you riding astride. You should have been put on a sidesaddle ages ago. I'm afraid I keep forgetting how old you are."

He looked in exasperation at his niece, noting as David would later that she had grown taller. For the first time he really saw the bone structure of her face, clear now that the childish softness of chin and cheeks had gone. With deep surprise he realized that Jane was going to be beautiful. All the more reason, he told himself firmly, for her to learn to conduct herself as a lady.

The Marquis of Rayleigh was at this time thirty-two years of age. He spent about half of the year in London and half of the year at Heathfield, with weeks set aside for visits to other great houses and sporting excursions. He was a good-

natured, easy-going man, whose one abiding interest in life was his horses. He liked his niece and
up to now he had approved of her. She was a
smashing rider; it was a pleasure to watch her
fearlessly take a steep jump or hold a nervous
thoroughbred to a collected canter. He had never
thought much about the fact that her life was ex-
cessively odd for a young girl of her class and expectations. Jane would inherit eighty thousand
pounds when she was twenty-one. She was a considerable heiress and would be expected to fill a
high position in society. As he looked at his niece,
dressed neatly in coat and well-worn breeches and
boots, her hair pulled back off her high-
cheekboned face, he felt a pang of guilt.

She was in a temper. Her extraordinary sea-
blue eyes flashed at him. "Enough, Jane," he said
firmly. "I blame myself for allowing you to run
wild for so long. You are growing into a young
lady, my dear. You must learn to act like one. You
are to ride a sidesaddle from now on, and that's an
end to it." He had terminated the argument by
leaving the room, and for the past six days had
held firm.

Jane was miserable. She had made one attempt
to ride the sidesaddle, taking one of the hunters
around the paddock for a few turns. She had returned to the stable in twenty minutes, her nostrils white with temper. "If I must ride this stupid
way, I would rather not ride at all," she announced to Tuft.

Every groom in the stable looked at her in

silent sympathy. There wasn't a man there who wouldn't have died for the small, imperious, black-haired child who stood before them, vibrating with misery and with anger.

She had been as good as her word. She hadn't ridden for four days now, and she was wretched. David, who was getting paid handsomely for his work this summer, had taken a few hours off to drive her out to their secret place.

He looked at her now in sympathetic comprehension. "You don't think Lord Rayleigh will change his mind?"

"No. All he does is say stupid things, like I have to learn to be a lady and behave like other girls. Well, I'm not like other girls!" Jane cried passionately.

"Of course you're not," he said matter-of-factly. With an easy movement he rose to his feet. "I've got to get back, Jane. Come along. I think I might have an idea."

He reached down to take her hand, pulling her somewhat unwillingly to her feet. She looked up at him, slightly resentful that he was growing so much taller than she. He was still slender, but the young body under the shirt and worn breeches was firm and hardened and had none of the awkwardness that often afflicts adolescents. At thirteen, three inches taller than he had been last year, David still never put a foot wrong.

"An idea?" she said hopefully. "What?"

But he refused to say, hustling her back through the woods to the gig that had been their transportation. When they reached the stables again, David put the sidesaddle on Centurian, one of the older hunters, and led him out to the paddock. Then David got into the saddle.

Jane leaned against the white railing, watching him go around. He finally stopped and called her over. She looked up at him and grinned.

"I know," he said good humoredly. "Look at this, Jane," he gestured to his right leg, crooked over the horn and resting securely in a high stirrup. "I'm virtually locked in," he said. "You'd never get thrown from a seat like this."

She put her hand on his leg and pushed. "I suppose not. But what has that got to do with anything?"

David jumped down. "I don't like it at all," he said with a worried frown. "It isn't safe. What would happen if you were out hunting and your horse fell?"

Jane stared at him a minute, then revelation dawned. "I would be trapped in the saddle," she said slowly. "The horse would fall right on me."

There was a tight look around David's firm mouth. "Bound to. Talk to your uncle about that, Jane. And Jane," he reached out to lightly touch her arm, "I'd accept a compromise if I were you."

For a long minute she stared rebelliously into the golden brown of David's eyes. His steady look never wavered. Then she heaved a sigh, nodded, and went off toward the house.

Lord Rayleigh was not at home, which gave Jane time to think through her approach. David had said she would have to compromise. Jane had long since realized that David was much more adept at dealing with people than she, so she pondered his suggestion seriously. She decided that she was prepared to learn *how* to ride sidesaddle, so long as she didn't have to actually *do* it.

Jane's attack on the sidesaddle as unsafe made a distinct impression on Lord Rayleigh. She had confronted him as he came in from a drive to the Hertforts' and, resignedly, he had taken her into the library.

"But, dash it, Jane, all women hunt sidesaddle," he protested.

"None of those women who were here last week did, Uncle Edward. Every single one of them turned back after fifteen minutes."

This was indisputably true. Women always came to hunt meets, but very few rode out with the men. It was too fast and rough for most women riders.

"I hope you don't expect me to stop hunting," Jane said indignantly.

Most men would not have hesitated to tell her that the hunting field was no place for a girl. Lord Rayleigh, who reverenced good horsemanship, could not do it. "No," he said slowly. "Of course you must hunt." He frowned. Now that he thought of it, what she had said was true. She'd never be thrown clear if she were riding in that damned saddle. The thing was a bloody death trap. He hesitated, looking at her worriedly.

"I'll make a bargain with you, Uncle Edward," Jane said in her cool, clipped voice.

He grinned. He couldn't help it. Any other girl would have coaxed and pleaded. Not Jane. "What bargain, brat?" he said.

"If I promise to learn to ride sidesaddle and to ride it on all formal occasions, may I continue to ride astride here at home?"

He thought for a minute. "I have one other condition."

She looked at him suspiciously. "What is that?"

"You must get yourself a skirt. Those breeches have to go."

There was a pause as Jane considered. "All right," she agreed. The Battle of the Sidesaddle was over.

There were repercussions, though. For the first time the Marquis began to think of his niece as a young girl. He was easy-going and careless, but once he thought about it he realized that Jane could not be allowed to continue as she was going. The next time he went up to London he consulted with Lady Carrington, a cousin in her forties who had young daughters of her own. The result of this discussion was that the following year Jane was sent to Miss Farner's Select Academy for Young Ladies in Queen Square, Bath.

Chapter V

Nothing can bring back the hour
Of splendour in the grass, of glory in the
    flower. . . .
                                —William Wordsworth

Jane hated school. She felt like a hawk in a cage;
the genteel, refined atmosphere of Miss Farner's
drove her into a hard and fierce isolation. The
other girls did not know how to deal with her.
The slender, aloof girl with her cold, clipped
voice and utter self-sufficiency puzzled them and
made them uneasy.

Jane was not defiant. She did as she was asked
and performed adequately at her studies. But her
light eyes had a faintly mocking look which disconcerted Miss Farner and often made her lose
the thread of whatever she was trying to say. Jane
was perfectly polite, but it was abundantly clear
to Miss Farner and to all her teachers that as far
as Jane was concerned, they might not have existed.

Miss Farner made one attempt to break
through the impenetrable reserve Jane had surrounded herself with. She called Jane into her pri-

vate sitting room one day about three months after Jane's arrival in Bath.

"Are you happy here, Lady Jane?" she inquired.

Jane's mouth set. "No," she answered, uncompromisingly.

"Why, may I ask?" Miss Farner's voice was scrupulously gentle. To have Lady Jane Fitzmaurice as a pupil was a feather in her bonnet; Miss Farner did not want to lose her.

"I don't want to be here. I don't belong here. There is nothing here for me." Jane sat upright on a chair, her back straight as always, her black head high.

"But why, Lady Jane?" Miss Farner persisted. "We want you to be happy. Won't you let us try to help you?"

Jane simply stared back, a derisive glint in her eyes. As if this stupid woman could do anything for her!

"Why don't you make friends with some of the other girls?" Miss Farner made one more attempt.

"I've already got a friend," Jane answered with finality. And that was that.

What saved Jane from her passive but absolute antagonism to Miss Farner's Select Academy and all who inhabited it was the advent of Miss Becker, the art mistress. Jane had always loved color; it gave her a pleasure that was purely aesthetic. Miss Becker gave Jane oil paints and taught her how to draw. It was her salvation. She went with Miss Becker to see all the paintings Bath had to offer the public. And she sat for hours at her easel, working with a hard concentration in her eyes, her black head on one side and an intense stillness over her whole figure.

So the days passed as she waited with rigid patience for the holidays, when she could go home and see David.

For David, too, life had changed irrevocably. At fifteen he went to work fulltime for the Marquis. His aunt's health was failing and it had been some years since Mr. Althorpe had been able to teach him anything David considered worthwhile. His aunt had bitterly opposed David's decision to become a stablehand. She had cherished secretly a hope that he would become a lawyer, like her father.

"There isn't money enough, Tante Héloise," David had said unarguably. "And besides, I shouldn't like it. I like working with horses. It's what I'm good at."

He was very good at it. In the spring of David's sixteenth year his aunt died and Tuft approached the Marquis on his behalf. "I'd like to train David to take my place, my lord," the old head groom said gruffly.

The Marquis had looked startled. "Take your place, Tuft? What do you mean?"

"I mean, my lord, that I'm getting old. I've saved my money and I'd like to retire in a few years. My sister has a nice cottage in Sussex, by the sea. She wants me to come and live with her."

The Marquis stared at the face of his faithful

retainer and realized with a shock that Tuft was indeed old. It didn't seem possible. Tuft had run the stables ever since the Marquis was a child; Heathfield without him was unthinkable. He cleared his throat. "You will have a handsome pension, Tuft, whenever you choose to leave. But this idea of training David! He is only a boy. Far too young for such a responsibility."

"David trained Dolphin, my lord," Tuft said simply.

The Marquis looked thunderstruck. "What?"

"Aye, my lord. I let him handle the whole program. He came to me once or twice with questions, but the credit for Dolphin must go to David." Dolphin was the Marquis's prime three-year-old, bred at Heathfield. He had won the Guineas at the Newmarket meeting two weeks ago.

"I can't believe it," the Marquis said slowly.

"It's true, my lord. The boy has a sixth sense about horses. I've never seen anything quite like it. It's as if he knows what they're feeling. I used to be sorry that he's grown so tall because it limits his uses as a rider. He is a very fine rider; but he will be a genius as a trainer."

"Will the grooms take orders from a sixteen-year-old boy?"

"The men will do anything for him. They like him, but they also respect him. They see the same thing in him that I do."

"I see," the Marquis said slowly. And so David

Chance, age sixteen, became the heir-apparent to the top racing stud in England.

That summer was the last one of the old Jane-and-David relationship. And even then, there were changes. David, who had always lunched with Jane at Heathfield during her holidays, now insisted on eating at his own cottage. He lived alone since his aunt had died, and Mrs. Copley, who had worked for Mlle. Dumont for years, continued to come every day to clean and to cook his dinner. Breakfast and lunch he did for himself. During that summer Jane took to going home with David for lunch. Privately, she felt it was much more comfortable since Mlle. Dumont was no longer there. At first, she would watch while David cooked; later, she would often do the meal herself.

David's scruples about coming to Heathfield had their origins in one main factor. As children he and Jane had always had their meals in the nursery; it was only this year that Jane had been allowed to dine downstairs. Eating with Jane was one thing, David felt, but eating in the Marquis's dining room was quite another. "It wouldn't be proper," he told Jane stubbornly.

Jane thought he was being ridiculous, but since she liked going to David's cottage better than eating under the eye of Miss Kilkelly in the nursery or McAllister, the Heathfield butler, in the dining room, she didn't pursue the point. On the whole she enjoyed her new status. Her Uncle Edward was much more interesting to talk to than Miss Kilkelly.

The Marquis enjoyed the change as well. She didn't come down when there was company, but she was infinitely preferable to dining alone. Since they both had a common passion, the conversation never lagged. And Jane had a caustic wit that the Marquis found genuinely amusing. In fact, he enjoyed the company of his fifteen-year-old niece more than the company of a large number of his acquaintances.

They were discussing Dolphin one evening when Jane broached the topic that had been on her mind for weeks. "You're running him this summer at Ascot, aren't you, Uncle Edward?"

"Yes. In the Gold Cup."

"And David is going?"

"As he is responsible for the horse, assuredly he is going."

Jane swallowed. "Then may I go, too?" she asked hopefully. She had always attended the racing meets at Newmarket, but the Marquis had never taken her to the meets at Epsom, Ascot, or any of the other tracks where his horses ran. On those occasions Lord Rayleigh had had no time for a child.

Now he looked speculatively at the slender girl facing him across the table. He saw her beautiful high cheekbones beneath eyes that were as blue-green as the sea; he saw her white, even teeth, chewing at the moment on a fresh-colored but slightly chapped lip; he saw her magnificent candle-straight hair, neatly parted and tied, schoolgirl-like, at her nape. She was not yet a woman, but she was no longer a child. "You would need a chaperone," he said slowly.

Jane's face lit. "Kelly will come," she said, breathless in her eagerness. "Oh, Uncle Edward, do let me come! This is the first horse that David has trained. Just think of how exciting it will be if he wins."

Looking at the bone-deep beauty of his niece's face, Lord Rayleigh felt a quiver of apprehension. "Do you ever think of anyone except David, Jane?" he asked casually.

"Of course I do," she answered, surprised. "I think about you. And about Miss Becker. And about the horses, naturally."

She was so transparently honest, he thought. Three people and a few horses: that was her world. She was still very much a child, after all. "Very well, Jane," he said. "You may come with me to Ascot."

Her eyes glowed like pale gems. "Thank you, Uncle Edward. I can't wait to tell David."

Lord Rayleigh had rented an entire inn for the summer meet at Ascot. His entourage on these occasions was usually all male, but this time he had made some exceptions. Jane had been allowed to come not entirely out of altruistic motives. The Marquis was thinking about getting married.

He was thirty-four years old, fifth Marquis of Rayleigh and head of the ancient Stanton family.

It was his duty to marry and produce an heir. He had procrastinated for many years, enjoying his free bachelor life, but he knew what was due to his position. Jane's future, too, was on his mind. A suitable husband would have to be found for her, and who better to handle that than his wife? So he had invited Lady Bellerman and her daughter Anne as well as his cousin Sophia Carrington and her husband to join his party at Ascot. Anne Bellerman was a prime candidate for the role of future Marchioness of Rayleigh. She was twenty years old, soft-spoken, even-tempered, and pretty. The Marquis thought he might live with her very comfortably. It wouldn't be a bad idea, at any rate, for her to meet Jane.

The Ascot meeting was to last five days. As Ascot was close to Windsor, the Prince of Wales usually entertained a large house party during that time; it was a social event as well as a race meet. An invitation to stay at Windsor or to join the parties of such famous noble owners as Lord Rayleigh was regarded as a social triumph. Very few of the beautiful women who appeared dutifully at the racetrack had come to see the horses.

For Jane, of course, the races were everything. The prestige, at age fifteen, of being included in the Marquis's party quite eluded her. She was allowed to join the company for dinner, although when the ladies retired to leave the men to their wine she went, not to the drawing room, but upstairs to bed.

It would have been an ordeal to many young

girls to be thrust into such sophisticated company; Jane felt quite comfortable. She had known many of the Marquis's friends, men like Lord Massingham and Mr. Firth and Sir Henry Graham, for years. She had hunted with them often. It never even occurred to her to feel shy.

Lady Carrington regarded Jane with considerable interest as they sat down to dinner the first night of the meet. Jane was dressed in a simple blue frock of schoolgirl cut and her hair was worn down her back, as befitted her age. But there was nothing of the *jeune fille* about Jane. She ate neatly with the appetite of a hungry schoolboy and all the time kept up a vigorous conversation with Lord Massingham, who was seated next to her. Lord Massingham was listening to her intently when she suddenly made a motion, as of a fencer thrusting home, and he threw back his head and laughed. My, my, Lady Carrington, cousin to both Lord Rayleigh and Jane, thought to herself; and she is only fifteen. She looked speculatively at the wide brow, high cheekbones, and square chin of the girl across the table. Edward will have his hands full with her, she thought with ironic amusement. And if he were planning to marrying the Bellerman girl, she would be no help in taming Jane. That black-haired child would ride roughshod right over the soft-spoken Anne.

Jane finished dinner utterly oblivious to the thoughts she had inspired in her cousin. She smiled vaguely upon the ladies as she left the drawing room to go upstairs. If she had met any one of them in another framework tomorrow, she wouldn't recognize her, but there was not a woman there who wouldn't have instantly known Jane.

David was staying at the stables with the horses and Jane spent most of her waking hours with him. The crowning moment of the whole meet came when Dolphin won the Gold Cup. The Marquis had invited David to join him for the race's running, and so both Jane and he had stood together along the rail in front of the Marquis's pulled-up carriage. Lord Rayleigh stood behind Jane, but she was conscious only of David. As the horses started she put out her hand and, without looking at her, David took it and held it tightly. When Dolphin came across the finish line a winner, the tight grip of his long fingers on hers told her all she needed to know about his feelings.

The Marquis turned from receiving the congratulations of his friends to hold out his hand to his young trainer. It gave Lord Rayleigh a shock to realize that he now had to look up to meet David's eyes. Several of the people who had been standing around came forward, anxious to meet the Marquis's new "wunderkind." David smiled and answered politely in his deep, gentle voice, then, at a break in the noise, he turned to the Marquis. "I think I will go see how Dolphin is doing, my lord," he said to Lord Rayleigh, but his eyes were on Jane. He felt a sudden need to get away from all these people, to be alone with her.

She nodded understandingly. "I'll come with you."

Laura Rivingdale stood beside the Marquis as the two of them moved off. She was staying with her husband at Windsor, but they had joined the Marquis for the race since they were part-time neighbors of his at Newmarket. Laura's long green eyes glinted as she watched David's blond-streaked head, easily visible over the crowd even though it was slightly bent toward the girl who walked beside him. "What an absolutely beautiful boy," she said softly, almost to herself.

The Marquis stared at her, his eyes slightly widened. "David?"

"Yes," she said. "David. How appropriate. One thinks of Michaelangelo."

"You must be mad, Laura," the Marquis said impatiently. "He is only sixteen years old."

She gave him a long, slow smile. "Age has nothing to do with it, Edward. Either you have that certain something or you don't." She tapped him lightly on the chest. "And your David most definitely has it." She walked away, leaving him staring after David and Jane, a troubled frown between his brows.

Chapter VI

But yet I know, where'er I go,
That there hath past away a glory from the earth.
—William Wordsworth

As Lord Rayleigh was beginning to realize, the gates of childhood were closing behind Jane and David. Even Jane, most oblivious of them all, was aware of changes. Dimly she understood that the old union of Jane-and-David was being threatened and, being Jane, she fought back. And, because other people had no importance to her, she assumed the change was emanating from David. They had always done things together; now he did things she was unable to do. He had reached his full growth of six feet two inches and his body, from hard work and exercise, was lean and hard. Jane felt he was leaving her behind and hated her few inches and lack of strength. She strove all through that summer to prove herself equal to him. Her silent struggle came to a head a week before she was due back at school.

The Marquis had recently purchased a new horse, an iron-gray stallion with a vicious temper. He wanted the horse primarily as a stud but planned to race him lightly, so he had to be kept

in the stable and exercised regularly. It usually
fell to David to ride him; very few of the grooms
could handle him. Jane had asked to try him once
and David had told her curtly that she wouldn't
be able to hold him.

Her eyes had flashed, but she hadn't challenged
him. She waited until he was not around one afternoon and then she entered the stable. "Saddle
Condottière for me," she said imperiously to one
of the younger grooms.

He gaped at her. "But, Lady Jane——"

"Don't argue with me," she said, her chin rising
ominously, "saddle him." Centuries of command
sounded in her clear voice.

"Yes, my lady," the groom mumbled, and went
to do her bidding.

She had been gone ten minutes when David returned. "Mr. David, Mr. David!" Stubbs, one of
the senior grooms, hastened to tell him. "Lady
Jane has taken Condottière out."

"What?" David's head snapped around quickly.
"When?"

"Ten minutes ago."

There was a white line around David's mouth.
"Where did she go?"

"To the heath, Mr. David."

"Get me Alexander," David said briefly, and
stood waiting while the black horse was saddled
and brought to him. He did not blame anyone for
allowing her to ride the gray. He knew Jane well
enough to guess what had happened. There were

two sharp lines between his brows and he did not look young at all.

He left the stableyard at a full gallop and came upon Jane five minutes later. She was having a hard time with Condottière. The gray horse wanted to run and Jane's arms and shoulders ached from trying to hold him to a slow gallop. Once he got hold of the bit she knew she would have a runaway. She was afraid, more for the horse than for herself, and the sound of galloping hooves behind her was very welcome. She gripped the reins tightly and in a minute Alexander was beside her and David had his hand on Condottière's bridle. The two horses slowed to a walk, then a halt. David swung out of the saddle and went to stand at Condottière's head. "Get down," he said roughly to Jane. Obediently she slid to the ground and went to take Alexander's reins from him. There was blood on her hands from where the reins had cut them. "Serves you right," he said tensely, his eyes on those hands. She opened her mouth to speak but he cut across her, "We are going back to the stable. Get up on Alexander." He waited until she was in the saddle, then mounted the great gray, turned him, and headed toward Heathfield without a backward glance to see if she was following.

She was. They arrived at the stable together and were met by most of the grooms, led by Tuft. David's mobile mouth was compressed. He waited for Jane to dismount, then said curtly, "Wait for me in the tack room." He led the gray horse into the stable and the grooms looked tentatively at Jane and waited for the explosion.

None came. She held her head high, but she walked to the tack room and closed the door behind her. Once she was safely inside she went to sit apprehensively in "their" corner. She had never seen David so angry.

No one else in the stable had ever seen him like this, either. They were used to Jane's tempers; they were almost proud of them. But David was another matter; he was always soft-spoken and calm, gentle and easy-going. They were more frightened of his grim mouth and the leaping light in his golden eyes than they ever were of Jane's fireworks.

David deliberately took his time with Condottière, hoping the familiar routine would help to calm him down. He wanted to shake Jane until her teeth rattled. When he finally opened the door to the tack room and saw her sitting so meekly waiting for him, his rage flared up once more.

"I could murder you," he grated between shut teeth.

Unexpectedly, she hung her head. "I'm sorry, David," she said low. "I was wrong. I won't ever do it again." She looked at him a trifle anxiously. "He wasn't hurt, was he?"

Outside the door the grooms, who had managed to find work in the immediate vicinity, exchanged looks of amazement. "Did you hear what I did?" Stubbs asked Holland.

"She said she was wrong," he replied in a dazed tone.

"All right, now," Tuft said briskly, having heard what he was most interested in, "get back to work, lads. Enough hanging about." They scattered to other areas of the stable, their opinion of David higher than ever.

Inside, David was saying furiously, "The hell with the bloody horse. Do you realize you might have killed yourself?"

Her sea-blue eyes widened slightly as she realized that his fury stemmed from concern for her. She stood quietly and let a torrent of words, all of which described her character in highly unflattering terms, pass unchallenged over her head. When he had finally run out of breath, she took a step closer to him. "I'm sorry," she repeated. "I was stupid. Forgive me, David."

He stared at her for a long moment, the force of his rage spent. Her ribbon had come loose and her black hair hung in a sheer mantle almost to her waist. Her eyes looked enormous and her mouth trembled slightly. He swallowed. "Let me see your hands," he said in a more normal tone. Obediently she came across to him and made no murmur as he cleaned and bound the ugly weals on her palms.

"Why did you do it?" he asked finally when he had put away the medical kit.

She refused to meet his eyes. "It was just . . . oh, I don't know." She made a vague gesture with her bandaged hand.

He looked at the shining black head, the top of

which reached just below his chin, and felt a sudden pain somewhere in the region of his heart. "Tell me," he said gently.

She looked up at him, her light eyes suddenly bright. "Oh, I wish I were a boy!" she cried passionately.

David's eyes were golden as he regarded the reed-slim figure before him. He put out a hand and touched her hair; it felt like soft silk. He noticed for the first time the beautiful way her head was set on her slender neck. Suddenly he was fiercely glad she was not a boy. He said as much, standing with his hand buried in the soft darkness of her hair. "I like you just the way you are. I don't want you to change at all."

Jane was oddly still as her great light eyes searched his face. "Really?" she said wonderingly.

"Really." There was no mistaking the utter sincerity of his tone.

She smiled, the enchanting smile she reserved only for him. "I feel better," she said.

Reluctantly he took his hand from her hair. "Good. I can take a few hours off this afternoon. Do you want to ride out to Marren Hill?"

"Yes. I would like that."

They left the tack room together as in accord with each other as usual. They both knew that something of importance had occurred between them, although neither was quite sure what it was.

The day before Jane left for school, George and

Laura Rivingdale rode over to Heathfield to see
the Marquis's new horse. The Rivingdales owned
a small stud some seven miles from Heathfield
and for the few weeks a year they were in
residence they were neighbors.

It was a crisp, sunny day when the Marquis appeared in the stableyard leading the Rivingdales.
David and Jane had been out on the heath with a
few of the grooms exercising the hunters and their
arrival in the yard coincided with the Marquis's.
The Marquis called to David and he came over,
handing his horse's reins to one of the grooms.

Laura Rivingdale looked at him and her eyes
narrowed. A lock of sun-bleached hair had fallen
forward over his forehead. His shirt was open and
she could see the golden-brown column of his
neck, the pulse beating strongly in the hollow of
his throat. There was about him a curious and almost godlike air of simplicity and directness. She
thought again of Michaelangelo. She asked him a
question about the horse and he replied, looking
at her in a friendly, unsmiling way.

Jane came up to them and exchanged greetings
in her cool, composed voice. "You've come to see
Condottière?" she said. "David had better bring
him out."

A corner of David's mouth twitched and he
gave her a half-glance, amused and tender. Laura
stared after him for a moment, then her eyes
turned, speculatively, to Jane. She was surprised
by what she saw. The plain child, who had so astonished the neighborhood by her riding prowess,

was growing up. Jane was beautiful. Laura's eyes moved from the striking face to the resilience and vigorous perfection of the young body, clothed so casually in an old riding outfit. Jane, unaware of her scrutiny, was talking easily with her uncle and Mr. Rivingdale, discussing the merits of the hunter she had been riding. David brought Condottière out and the great gray was duly admired by the assembled company. Before they left, Laura Rivingdale ascertained that Jane was leaving for school the next day. She found this piece of information extremely interesting.

Chapter VII

Doth she not think me an old murderer,
Now I have stain'd the childhood of our joy. . . .
—William Shakespeare

Jane returned to school for her last year. This
September she was almost looking forward to going back. She had worked all summer on a
painting that she was anxious for Miss Becker to
see.

Jane's position at school had changed radically
in the three years she had been there. The dis-
trust and uneasiness of her first year had given
way to genuine admiration. Jane Fitzmaurice suf-
fered from none of the uncertainties or insecuri-
ties that beset most adolescent girls. She went her
way with a sublime disregard of either the cus-
toms or conventions that held the other girls in
bondage. She was totally uninterested in romance,
a topic that loomed large in the minds and the
conversations of the other girls; yet no one was
oblivious to the fact that the dancing master and
the Italian master looked upon Jane with obvious
admiration. She treated them with the arctic
aloofness she reserved for anyone she did not
greatly care for. The intensity of her feelings for

David preserved her from the schoolgirl fantasies of her fellow students. She was both more innocent and more mature than they.

She waited two days before she mentioned her painting to Miss Becker. The art mistress asked to see it immediately and Jane brought it down to the small art room which was, blessedly, empty of everyone but themselves. She propped the canvas up on an easel by the window and stepped back, her eyes on Miss Becker's face, her brows tense with anticipation.

The woman's eyes widened as she looked at the painting before her. It was a picture of a boy and a horse standing in the middle of a grassy heath. What made it so extraordinary was the quality of the light she had achieved. It was a golden picture, full of the pure light of sun and sky and meadow. The boy, brown and gold as a young god, stood quietly holding the glossy chestnut horse whose coat reflected the light of the sun. It was dazzling, yet it was curiously peaceful, Miss Becker thought. Just so must the world have looked before the fall.

She turned to Jane, a look almost of reverence on her face. "It is beautiful, Jane. But you knew that."

Jane's face relaxed. "I thought it was good," she said cautiously.

"It is more than good. You are a painter, my dear."

"No," Jane contradicted. "I'm not a painter yet. But someday I will be."

"You are one now." Miss Becker looked again at the painting. "There are some techniques you have still to learn, but your use of color is extraordinary." She looked at Jane curiously. "What are you going to do with this?"

"Give it to David for his birthday."

"Is that David in the picture?" Miss Becker was the only one at Miss Farner's who knew anything about him.

"Yes."

"He is beautiful."

"Yes," said Jane matter-of-factly. "I think so."

The Christmas holidays came and Jane was at Heathfield to give David his picture on his seventeenth birthday, which was two days after Christmas day. Then she returned to school and winter set in. On February twelfth, Laura Rivingdale returned to Hailsham Lodge, having become extremely bored with her husband and children, all of whom were at their main residence near Canterbury in Kent. She had thought of going to London, but the idea of London in February was blighting. It did not take her long to decide that Newmarket would be more amusing.

When her husband expressed surprise at her decision, she simply shrugged and said she needed to get away. He suspected she had a new lover and, since he had a new mistress he wanted the freedom to pursue, he made no objections to her going.

Laura Rivingdale was a very beautiful woman

and at the moment she was very bored. She was tall and statuesque, with slanting green eyes and lovely, tawny hair. She had married George Rivingdale when she was eighteen and had given him two sons. After that she felt she had done her duty and they both looked elsewhere for their pleasures. The children were being reared by a nursemaid at their home in Kent.

She came to Newmarket because she could not forget David's face. When she rode over to Heathfield, it was to discover that Jane had returned to school and the Marquis was at a houseparty at Bellerman Hall. She managed to run down David in the stables. He was courteous, although he obviously had no idea what it was she wanted. She left after a few minutes, her image of him only reinforced by the flesh-and-blood reality. He looked curiously innocent and pure, she thought. Really beautiful. She was very glad she had come.

David didn't give her a thought. He went home after dark as he did every night and found his dinner simmering in the oven. He lit the candles and went to see what Mrs. Copley had left him to eat. As he was setting the table he heard the door open. He looked up and saw Laura Rivingdale.

She came into the room and closed the door behind her. "I was lonely all by myself in that great house," she said. "I thought I'd come and talk to you."

He didn't ask her why she had come to Newmarket alone. He didn't point out the number of servants at the Lodge. He simply laid the fork on the table and said quietly, "I see."

She took off her cloak and came forward into the light of the fire. She looked very lovely. "I have been thinking of you, David," she said softly.

"Have you?" He hadn't moved, and his still beauty drew her like a magnet.

"Yes," she murmured huskily. She was tall, but she had to reach up quite a long way to pull his head down to meet hers. He remained perfectly still for a minute, with her mouth on his, as if he were holding his breath. Then his arms came up to encircle her and draw her closer. After a long moment she pulled back from him and looked up meeting his eyes, golden now with desire. "Let's go into the bedroom," she said.

"All right," he answered, and held the door for her to precede him.

Laura stayed on at Newmarket for several months. She told her husband and her interested friends that she had not been feeling well and her doctor had prescribed quiet and regular exercise, both of which she was getting at Hailsham Lodge. In reality she could not tear herself away from David.

For the first time in her life Laura found herself emotionally involved with a man; that the man was seventeen years old was one of life's ironies, she thought. Several times she tried to explain to herself what it was about David that so held her. It was, she decided, a quality of tenderness that she had never found in any other man. Perhaps it came, she thought, from his working so much with animals.

She was endlessly curious about him. He looked as if he should be up at Oxford or Cambridge with the sons of nobles and gentlemen, not exercising horses in someone else's stable. There was nothing coarse about him; he was clearly cut and defined from his chiseled face and sensitive, mobile mouth to his fine, narrow, strong hands.

"Who were your parents?" she had asked him curiously a week after their first encounter.

"They were French," he answered readily. "My father was the steward for a noble family in Artois. He was killed protecting his employer's property during the revolution. My mother died shortly after him. My aunt took me out of France and brought me to England when I was one."

She looked at him, a puzzled frown between her brows. They were in bed and he was lying on his back, his hands clasped behind his head. The fire lit up his streaked blond head and long, golden lashes. He did not look at all French. She said as much.

A slow, terribly attractive smile came over his eyes and brows, although his mouth remained grave. "All the members of one nationality do not necessarily resemble each other," he said gently.

There was a slight pain inside her chest as she looked at him. "You are so *beautiful*," she murmured in her throat.

At that he did laugh. "And so are you," he replied, and reached for her once again.

She could not get enough of him. He was tender. He was patient. He was passionate. He was the best lover she had ever had. He was seventeen years old. He did not love her.

It was the knowledge of this last fact that hurt her the most. He was kindness itself; he would never want to hurt her, but the sight of him, beautiful and, ultimately, inaccessible, did hurt her. It had begun very shortly after her arrival in Newmarket. She had seen Jane's painting hanging over the mantel in David's cottage and had asked him about it.

"It is magnificent. Who did it?"

There was a tiny pause. "Jane," he finally said.

"Jane?" She turned to him in surprise. "I didn't know Jane could paint like this."

He had looked at her in a way that was unmistakable and had changed the subject. He did not want to talk about Jane.

As the weeks and months went by, the shadow of that unspoken name hung like poison over Laura's mind. It drove her wild that he refused to speak about Jane. Every time Laura tried to introduce her name into the conversation, David would give her an inimical stare that said clearly "No Trespassers." It was Jane who stood between them; it was Jane who gave him that look of untouched purity that she found so agonizingly attractive; it was Jane he loved.

Spring came and still Laura was at Hailsham Lodge. In a few weeks, Jane would be home from school and David found himself in a dilemma. He wished Laura would go, but he didn't know how to tell her. He wasn't quite clear about his own feelings, but one thing he was sure of: he never wanted Jane and Laura to meet. He never wanted Jane to know about Laura. In some obscure way he felt he had betrayed Jane and the feeling made him uncomfortable. He began to avoid the cottage, staying on later and later at the stables on the pretense of hard work.

But when he returned home late one evening, she was there. He came in quietly, acknowledging her presence at his table with a brief nod. He went right to the stove and stirred the simmering stew.

"It's rabbit," Laura said tightly.

"Good," he said. "I'm hungry." But he made no motion to dish out the food. He turned, leaned his shoulders against the wall, and looked at her gravely. Laura saw something in his still face that frightened her. She took a breath and hurried into talk, trying to forestall him, to head off whatever it was he was going to say to her.

He let her go on without interruption and when she finally ran down said, as if she had not spoken at all, "It's no good, Laura. We must stop seeing each other." His voice was so soft and so final that she went very still.

"Can you tell me why, David?" she said at last, her voice sounding breathless.

"There are many reasons," he replied easily. "Your husband is one of them. So is Lord Rayleigh. He would not be at all pleased to discover that his trainer was having an *affaire* with the wife of one of his friends." His pronunciation of the word *affaire* was distinctly French.

She clenched her hands. "Is it because Jane is coming home?"

He stared at her, hating her, hating the sound of Jane's name on her lips. "Yes," he finally said tensely, "it is because Jane is coming home."

She was taut as a strung bow. He had hurt her, now she wanted to hurt him. "They will never let you near her, stableboy," she flung at him. "They'll marry her off to some great lord and you'll never see her again."

His eyes were pure gold, his nostrils pinched and white, his mouth thinned with anger. "I don't think of Jane that way," he said coldly.

She prepared to leave. "Yes, you do," she told him brutally. "But your great love will get you exactly nowhere. Rayleigh will see to that." She left the cottage, slamming the door behind her, and the next day she left Newmarket for London.

Chapter VIII

It is my lady, O, it is my love!
Oh, that she knew she were!
—William Shakespeare

David's whole life belonged to Jane. Now Laura's words threatened the security of his love. Over and over again they replayed themselves in his brain. "They'll marry her off to some great lord and you'll never see her again." After Laura left, he had automatically gone about his nightly chores, forcing himself to eat some of the stew, washing up the dishes, and mending the fire. When he could think of nothing else to do, he went and sat down on the edge of his bed. The words drove back into his memory, brutal and inescapable. "You'll never see her again." He buried his face in his hands. He was still sitting there when the fire burned out.

In the two weeks that remained before Jane's arrival, David sought to stave off his fears. Jane was still young, he told himself. They could not possibly think of marriage for her for years. He never questioned the purity of his own love; he had never felt for Jane what he had felt for Laura Rivingdale. It did not occur to him that his ex-

61

perience with Laura would radically alter the way
he looked at Jane.

Jane had been home for two days when she arrived in the stableyard with a picnic lunch and
some fishing poles. "You can take an afternoon off
from your labors," she told David. "Let's go fishing."

He hesitated a minute, then capitulated. "All
right, I'll get the gig."

They drove out, heading for their secret place
without even discussing their destination. It was
automatic. They always went there when Jane
came home.

They spoke lazily. Jane was content because she
was with David, and he was absorbed by his own
new thoughts. They tied the horse and gig in the
woods and proceeded by foot along the narrow
path that led to the lake. Jane went first and
David watched her walking, comparing this summer's Jane to the Jane of last year. Her old,
much-washed muslin dress moved easily with her
body. He noticed for the first time her slim,
supple waist, the curve of hip that tapered to
long, slim legs. He swallowed. She would be seventeen in October, he thought.

They emerged from the trees into the sunlight
and Jane laughed delightedly. "Now I really know
I'm home," she turned to him, her extraordinary
eyes alight. "Whenever I feel I can't bear Bath for
one more minute, when I know that if one more
silly girl chatters at me I shall *scream*, I run to my
room and close my eyes and pretend I'm here."

"Do you really, Jane?" he asked curiously. "And does it help?"

"Yes. I feel peaceful again. As though I were armored against the world and no one could bother me anymore."

He stared at her intently. "Why is that, do you think?"

She frowned a moment, in concentration. "I'm not sure," she said slowly. "I think it's because this is *our* place. Nobody but us has ever been here. Heathfield is associated with many people, but here there is only the two of us. It's our safe place, I guess. No one can get at us here."

He suddenly said fiercely, "Do you remember the time you said you wished we could stay here always?"

She nodded, surprised be his uncharacteristic vehemence. "Yes. I remember."

"Sometimes I wish it, too."

She looked up at him, a puzzled expression on her face. "Has something happened, David? You sound strange."

"Why?" he said tightly. "Is it strange of me to want to be with you?"

"No," she answered consideringly. "But other people have never bothered you the way they bother me. You get along with people better. You never feel out of place, like I do at school."

He looked at her face with its patrician bones and he began to laugh. "I fail to see how people can bother you, Jane, when as far as I can see you simply ignore most of them. And you feel out of place at school because you feel superior. I have never had that luxury."

She put her head on one side and looked at him through narrowed lashes. "What you say of me might be true, David Chance, but I've felt inferior to you, which is more than you can say about me." Having delivered what she thought was a home thrust, Jane smiled brilliantly. "Come on, let's eat. I'm starving."

"You're always starving," he said automatically as he followed her closer to the lake, but his thoughts were far away. Stableboy, Laura had called him. They'll never let you near her, she had said. He avoided looking at Jane as they sat sharing the food she had brought. He was afraid of what she would read in his eyes.

After lunch they both fished. David caught two middle-sized fish immediately and decided to give up. Jane was determined to catch something and stayed on while he went back to stretch out on the grass. His thoughts were mixed as he watched her nimble, vigorous figure moving about on the rocks. Her skirt was kilted up and he could see the perfect oval shape of her kneecaps. The slender calf and high-arched instep were as familiar to him as his own hard-muscled horseman's legs. She had a small half-moon-shaped scar behind her right knee. He saw it in his mind's eye; he was too far away from her for it to be visible now. He stared for a long time at the slender, proud body, a body he had watched every year as it grew in beauty, and some deep-buried feeling began to stir within him.

There was a shout of triumph from the lake and Jane was coming toward him waving a fish whose scales glinted in the sun. She sank to the ground beside him and pulled the ribbon from her hair. It rippled around her, blue-black in the bright sunlight. He reached out briefly to touch it. "I love your hair," he said.

"It's not stylish. It doesn't curl. They want me to cut it," she answered.

"Don't."

"Not if you don't want me to," she answered agreeably.

"I don't."

"All right." She smiled at him. It was the smile she reserved for him only. It had been his property for years. Why now should the blood suddenly start pounding in his veins? There were tiny beads of sweat on her forehead and neck. She swung her hair forward over her shoulder and began to plait it. David jumped to his feet and started to collect their things. "What are you doing?" she asked, surprised.

"I have to get back," he replied curtly.

"But, David," she was beginning when he cut in across her words.

"I don't own Heathfield stables, Jane, I am only employed to help run them. I can't take hours off at a time to go picnicking."

She stared at him in bewilderment, sensing hostility that she did not understand. She opened her mouth to argue, but the face she was looking at was set and stern. She rose effortlessly to her feet and began to help him gather their belongings. When they were all packed into the bag she had brought, he turned into the woods leaving Jane to follow with the fishing gear.

Her eyes were on David's back as they moved along the narrow path and she did not even see the root that tripped her up. With a cry she was flung to her knees; the fishing poles went flying as she broke her fall with her hands.

In a minute David was beside her, his face white under its tan. "Jane! Are you all right?"

Her mouth was twisted in pain. "My ankle, David. Oh God, I think I've broken it."

She had rolled to a sitting position and the movement sent shooting pains through her ankle. Unceremoniously, he knelt at her feet, pushed her skirt up, and untied her light sandal. Her unblemished, straight-toed foot and slender ankle looked perfectly normal. He touched it lightly and she winced.

"You probably sprained it," he said soothingly. "Come on, I'll carry you to the gig. Once you get home, we can send for Dr. Jarman."

She nodded and obediently raised her arms to him. He lifted her easily and her arms slid naturally around his neck. Her head felt dizzy and she buried her face in his shoulder. He could feel her breasts pressed against him; the thin fabrics of her dress and his shirt were very little barrier. She took a long, deep breath. He was conscious only of her warm, slim body in his arms. It was not a child's body anymore.

They reached the gig and with mingled reluctance and relief he deposited her on the seat. When he swung up beside her, she clutched his arm. "Do you really think it's just sprained?" she asked anxiously.

He looked into her fear-darkened eyes and suddenly the gate to their childhood opened again. In so many ways Jane was brave as a lion, but she was afraid of being sick or injured. She enjoyed good health, strength, and agility and was terrified of any threat to her physical well-being. And she always thought the worst. So now he laughed naturally. "You baby," he said good-naturedly. "I'm pretty sure it's not broken, but if it is, it will heal up. Stop making such an ass of yourself."

"But I'll be wrapped up like a mummy!" she wailed.

"Stow it, Jane," he recommended. "You'll probably be back in the saddle next week."

His lack of sympathy had the same bracing effect on her that it always had in such circumstances. "You're totally heartless," she accused him, her attention diverted from her injuries to his attitude.

"If you mean I'm heartless enough not to agree with you that a head cold is pneumonia and a sore throat is diptheria, then you're right," he responded immediately.

"Just because you're never sick or hurt. . . ."

"I am, too," he retorted. "Only I don't make great dramatic scenes about it."

"Of course not, you're just perfect, aren't you?" Jane said hotly.

They were back in the country of their childhood, united in an argument they were both familiar and comfortable with. Unfulfilled love and unspoken longing had nothing to do with them. For the space of that ride they were Jane-and-David once again. But it was a felicity that could not last.

David was not a child anymore. Although he fought against the knowledge, he was forced to realize over the course of that summer that his feelings for Jane had altered. His love had always been the one great constant of his life. It was not something he thought about. It was simply there, unnoticed and essential, like the air he breathed. Jane's absences at school had been bearable because he had always known she was coming back. It had never occurred to him that there would be a time when she would not.

It had not yet occurred to her. Nor did she realize his sudden, painful awareness of her physical beauty and desirability. Jane had never read a romantic novel in her life and the girls at school had never tried to confide their own adolescent yearnings into her sublimely indifferent ears. Motivated, perhaps, by an instinct for self-preservation, she clung fiercely and blindly to childhood.

To her they were still Jane-and-David. But to David the love that had always been the foundation of his happiness had begun to be the cause of a profound desolation.

Chapter IX

Full soon thy Soul shall have her earthly freight,
And custom lie upon thee with a weight. . . .
—William Wordsworth

In August, Jane and the Marquis were to go on a visit to Bellerman Hall. Lord Rayleigh's engagement to Miss Anne Bellerman had been officially announced some months ago and the wedding was set for October.

Jane thought the whole business of protocol surrounding the wedding to be a deadly bore. "First we go there for a week," she told David, "then they come here. Then we all go back there for the wedding. I thought at last I'd have a chance to spend autumn at home, instead of in that dreadful school, and now I have to trip around the countryside making wedding visits."

She sounded so disgusted that David had to smile. "I hope you show a more cheerful face to Lord Rayleigh."

She sighed. "I try to. Uncle Edward is a dear, and if he wants to marry Anne Bellerman, then I'll certainly do my part."

They were sitting in the stable office. Outside the rain was pouring down and consequently the afternoon gallops had been called off. David was taking five of the horses to the meet at Epsom next month. Lord Rayleigh would not be going himself, as he was committed to prewedding visits. Jane would miss the races also and, although she made an heroic attempt to appear gracious about accompanying the Marquis, she would have much preferred to go with David.

"What is Miss Bellerman like?" David asked curiously.

"Very gentle. Easy to handle. Docile disposition."

"Jane!" David's sherry-colored eyes were alight with laughter. "You really must stop talking about people as if they were horses."

"Nonsense. It's a great compliment. I don't like most people half as well as I like most horses."

He gave a gentle tug to the black plait that hung down her back almost to her waist. "Idiot," he said. "Do you like her?"

"Anne, do you mean?"

"Yes."

"She's all right, I guess. I suppose Uncle Edward has to get married. The succession and all that, I mean. She's probably the best he could come up with from our point of view."

David was staring at her. He had lately become extremely sensitive to Jane's obtuseness. Her cold-blooded analysis of her uncle's marriage rather shocked him. He blinked. "Our point of view?" he questioned finally.

"Yes. She won't come messing around where

she's not wanted. As I said before, she's very easy to handle. Once she's here, life should go on exactly as it always has. Only now, hooray, hooray, I don't have to go back to school."

With difficulty he dragged his eyes from her satisfied face. She was such a child, he told himself. She seemed to have no idea that the fact that she was no longer a schoolgirl was itself the sign of a changing future. He switched the subject and began to talk about the coming meet.

Bellerman Hall was in Bedfordshire, so Jane and Lord Rayleigh did not have long to travel. The Marquis was anxious for Jane and Anne to become better acquainted. He thought that Anne, so sweet and feminine, could exercise a beneficial influence on his niece. He was acutely aware that it was his duty to see Jane properly married, and he realized she needed a good deal of female guidance before she would be ready to make her debut into society. Fortunately, he was sublimely unaware of Jane's opinion of his intended bride.

"I think you will like Miss Bellerman very much, Jane," he said as their carriage rolled up the wide drive leading to Bellerman Hall.

"I liked her very much the few times I met her," Jane said politely. She was genuinely fond of the Marquis and was perfectly willing to make herself pleasant to the insipid Anne if it would please him.

The carriage came to a halt at the great front entrance and two footmen leaped to open the door for them. By the time they had alighted the front door had opened and a starched major domo arrived to lead them to Lord and Lady Bellerman, their host and hostess.

Lady Bellerman sent one of her maids to help Jane dress for dinner that evening, and the woman exclaimed when she saw the magnificent fall of black hair that Jane was brushing. "How do you wear it, Lady Jane?" the woman asked, lifting the silky weight in one hand.

"I usually just tie it back," Jane answered carelessly.

"That is all right for a schoolgirl, Lady Jane, but you are a young lady now. It must be worn up."

Jane shrugged. "It won't curl. And I won't cut it. If you can do anything with it, you're welcome to try."

Lady Bellerman's Rose had a burning aspiration to be a lady's personal dresser one day and she went to work on Jane with unaffected zeal. When Jane saw herself in the mirror after Rose had finished, her eyes widened in astonishment. Her hair had been drawn off her face and coiled in impeccable fashion at the back of her head. The style made her look much older; it emphasized her magnificent cheekbones and long-lashed, light eyes. Her neck, unencumbered by its usual weight, looked delicate and lovely as it rose from her modest blue evening dress. "I look so different," she said.

"You look lovely, Lady Jane," Rose told her sin-

cerely. "Here." She took a spray of white roses
from the vase on a table and tucked them into
Jane's hair.

"Well, thank you, Rose," Jane said, casting a
doubtful look at her reflection once more. She
shrugged briefly and turned to the door, effec-
tively banishing her appearance from her mind.
She needed to brace herself to be polite to a whole
collection of Bellermans who had been assembled
to meet her uncle and herself.

They sat down eighteen to dinner. Jane was
placed between Anne's uncle, Mr. Francis Addington, and her eldest brother, Mr. John Bellerman.
Both gentlemen eyed her with delight and vyed
energetically for her attention. Jane thought Mr.
Addington, who was one of the shining lights of
the dandy set, ridiculous. However, she dutifully
smiled at his practiced patter, stared somewhat
haughtily at his profuse compliments, and gener-
ally speaking impressed him as being remarkably
sophisticated for her age. She enjoyed her conversation with Mr. John Bellerman much more. He
knew through his sister that Jane was an avid
rider, and as soon as he had her attention he said,
"I hear you like to ride, Lady Jane."

Jane never knew what to reply to statements
like that. It was as if someone had commented
that he heard she liked to breathe. Mr. Bellerman
met her amazed stare and hurried on, "If you like,
I'll show you some very good runs tomorrow."

Jane's smile was positively kindly. Any chance
she had to get away from this clutch of Beller-

mans seemed like manna in the desert. "How lovely," she said crisply. Then, remembering her duty, she glanced to where her uncle was courteously conversing with an ancient Bellerman aunt. "That is, if Uncle Edward says it's all right," she amended.

"I'll talk to him," John Bellerman promised. He too had been looking with dread toward these wedding visits. It seemed fantastic luck to find that the Marquis's niece, who apparently filled his gentle sister with such dread, was in fact the most stunningly beautiful girl he had ever seen.

After dinner the ladies retired to the drawing room and Jane was subjected to a barrage of aunts and cousins who questioned her with ruthless intent. Feeling extremely virtuous, she kept a firm hold on her temper and answered with regal serenity. She made the ladies rather uneasy.

When the gentlemen rejoined them, Anne was asked to play on the pianoforte. She played very nicely and Jane looked approvingly at her fair head and pretty face. It would be fine with her if Anne spent the whole of her day at the piano.

Unfortunately, Mr. Addington then insisted that Lady Jane give them an example of her talents. She looked despairingly at the Marquis, whose long mouth twitched in amused sympathy, but he said inexorably, "I'm sure Jane will be delighted to play for you."

Jane arose, weary resignation in every line of her lithe young body. "If you insist," she murmured sweetly. "I would suggest that any true music lovers leave the room, however." She then sat down and performed a perfectly correct Mozart sonata. She made no errors, but the performance was wooden and uninspired. When she had finished, Jane turned and faced the company. "I save my genius for the hunting field," she said with perfect composure and relinquished her seat to Anne.

On the whole, the visit went exceedingly well. Anne had invited Jane to walk with her in the garden one afternoon and the two girls found they got along surprisingly well. Anne had been terrified of Jane. She knew the Marquis expected her to chaperone his niece. She knew also that he was very fond of Jane. But from what he said of her, Anne had gotten the picture of a self-willed, self-confident Amazon. Jane's alarming self-possession whenever they had met previously had intimidated Anne, also. She did not quite see how she was going to have the nerve to take Jane in charge.

Closer acquaintance proved to be reassuring. Jane was on her best behavior and entered into all of Anne's schemes and ideas with flattering attention. They also had a very satisfactory time tearing apart the characters of the assorted aunts and cousins Lady Bellerman had gathered to plague them with.

In fact, to their mutual surprise, both girls found themselves inclined to like one another. Anne obviously cared for the Marquis, which Jane thought was a sign of intelligence on her part. She showed no signs at all of wanting to change him, which Jane appreciated immensely. She was not a person who adapted to change easily, and the Marquis was one of the steady markers in her life. She wanted him to stay exactly as he was. She was grateful to Anne for her apparently identical wish.

Lord Rayleigh was pleased as well with the harmony that reigned between his fiancée and his niece. He was also pleased with Jane's social performance. Apparently she was not as backward in that area as he had feared. He had not missed the admiring looks of Mr. Addington or the apparent infatuation of young Mr. Bellerman. He wouldn't be at all surprised, he thought with some pride, if Jane turned out to be a great success.

Chapter X

Whither is fled the visionary gleam?
Where is it now, the glory and the dream?
— William Wordsworth

Jane cared about very few people, but to those few she was fanatically loyal. It was this quality of loyalty that made her so popular with all the servants at Heathfield. She had temper tantrums and expected her orders to be obeyed without question, but if any member of the staff had a serious problem they never hesitated to seek her out. There wasn't a person working in the house or in the stables who didn't remember vividly how she had unhesitatingly handed over a whole quarter's allowance to pay the fine for one of the grooms who had unfortunately found himself brought up before a magistrate for unseemly conduct at a race meet. Or how she instantly summoned the Marquis's own physician to attend any servant who was ill or hurt.

Consequently, there was very little change in the staff at Heathfield. Jane was usually surrounded with familiar faces there, a state of affairs that was necessary to her serenity. She was only truly comfortable with people she knew and, aside from

David, the person she knew best in the world was the Marquis. Jane, who could be so incredibly oblivious to most of the human race, was quite sensitive to the feelings of those few people who mattered to her. She knew it was important to the Marquis that she like Anne. She knew it was important to him that the wedding plans should go smoothly. She knew also that he did not love Anne; her assessment of the marriage that had so shocked David had been, in fact, quite accurate. She knew, finally, that the Marquis did love her, and with the loyalty that so endeared her to the household, she grimly determined to do everything in her power to help him through one of the most important events in his life.

So when he told her that Lady Bellerman had invited her to remain at Bellerman Hall for the month's duration of his honeymoon, she had not flared up at him.

"That is very nice of her, Uncle Edward," she had said politely, "but I would rather come back here."

He sighed. "I know you would, Jane. But Lady Bellerman is quite adamant that it would not be proper for you to remain here by yourself with only the servants."

Jane's eyes flashed white lightning. "Not proper? What does she mean?"

The Marquis looked at her soberly. "Jane, my dear, listen to me. You are a young lady now. You are not a child anymore. There are many things that are acceptable for a child that are not acceptable for a young lady. Besides," he hurried on as he saw her mouth begin to open, "it's only for a month. Just until Anne and I get back from our honeymoon. Then we will all come back to Heathfield for Christmas."

The worried look in his eyes was not lost on Jane. Her lips compressed. "Very well, Uncle Edward," she said finally. "I will stay at Bellerman Hall for November."

He looked at her for a moment and his eyes were suddenly warm with affection. "You're a good girl, brat," he said. "I appreciate it."

The Marquis was in fact worried about Jane's staying at Heathfield without him, but not for the reasons of propriety put forward by Lady Bellerman. He was worried about David.

Jane's friendship with David was of such long duration that the Marquis regarded it as perfectly natural and acceptable, as did everyone else connected with Heathfield. If he had been questioned, he would have unhesitatingly said they were like brother and sister; it had simply never occurred to him that the friendship between those two children could ever flare up into something infinitely more powerful than the uncomplicated comradeship they had shared for years.

However, he was beginning to wonder if he had been guilty of a grave misjudgment. The first jolt to his complacency had come when the Bellerman family arrived at Heathfield for a visit in September. Lord Rayleigh's cousin, Lady Carrington, was kind enough to act as official hostess since Jane was still too young for such an onerous responsibility. Lady Carrington engaged to take care of the older members of the party; Jane's job was to see to the entertainment of Anne and her brother John. Since Jane's idea of entertaining someone was to put them on a horse, they spent a lot of time in the saddle and at the stables. And, naturally, they saw quite a bit of David.

One evening after dinner the Marquis had taken Anne for a stroll in the garden and she broached a subject that was clearly troubling her. "If you don't mind my asking, my lord," she said in her soft voice, "just who is David Chance?"

He looked at her, a trifle puzzled. "David? My trainer, you mean?"

"Yes." Anne hesitated. "He is not exactly what one expects in a groom, is he? He speaks like a gentleman. He looks like a gentleman, too."

The Marquis frowned. "He is a gentleman," he said somewhat shortly. "His parents were respectable French people who had the misfortune to fall foul of the revolution. His aunt got him out of the country, but they lost most of their money. He was educated with Jane. He works for me because he needs to earn a living and because he is a genius with horses."

"I don't mean to anger you, my lord," Anne said gently. "I'm sure he is a fine boy. I just wonder if it is wise to allow Jane to spend so much time with him."

Lord Rayleigh shrugged slightly. "My dear Anne, Jane and David have been inseparable since they were children. They are extremely attached to one another. I can hardly tell her that it is not proper for her to spend time with her best friend."

"I might perhaps hint," she began diffidently, but the Marquis cut her off with a shout of laughter.

"I beg your pardon, Anne," he said when he had recovered himself. "But the thought of hinting to Jane. . . ." Amusement trembled in his voice again. "Tact and indirection will never work with Jane," he said finally, and his eyes now were sober. "Your comments would either pass completely over her head or she would catch you up and demand to know what you were talking about. She has many faults, but there are two things about her you can always count on: her honesty and her loyalty."

Anne felt snubbed. "I'm sorry if I have offended you, my lord," she said stiffly.

"You haven't offended me," he answered, "but you would offend Jane if you tried to tell her that it was not socially acceptable for her to see David."

"I wasn't worried about the social acceptability," she said defensively, conscious of the need to justify herself.

He stopped dead and looked at her impatiently. "Then what *are* you worried about, Anne?"

She looked at him straightly. If he admired honesty, he should have it. "You want me to find Jane a husband, my lord, or so you have said."

"Yes?"

"Well, that might prove rather difficult when her dearest friend just happens to be the most beautiful man I have ever seen in my life. If Jane starts to compare her prospective suitors to David, we might find ourselves in the middle of a very unpleasant situation."

He continued to stare at her, but now there was a definite frown between his black brows. "Nonsense, Anne," he said finally. "He's been a big brother to her, that's all."

She drew her shawl more closely around her shoulders. "Perhaps you are right, my lord. After all, you know her much better than I do. It is getting a trifle chilly; shall we go in and join the others?"

He agreed with instant solicitude and escorted her back through the open French windows. She had done her duty, Anne thought to herself. She personally thought the Jane-David relationship was extremely dangerous, but she was not going to raise the subject anymore. She would not again make the mistake of seeming to criticize Jane.

Anne had been more effective than she realized. Lord Rayleigh was so much in the habit of regarding Jane and David as children that he had tended to ignore all evidence to the contrary. And there was a great deal of evidence to the contrary, he realized as he began to think about it. The Marquis had heard rumors about Laura Rivingdale.

He began to watch Jane and David with a care-

ful eye, and the day before the Bellermans were
due to leave for Bedfordshire he organized an ex-
pedition into Bury St. Edmunds to see the famous
abbey where the English barons had gathered to
swear they would force King John to give his as-
sent to the Magna Carta. As the weather was
warm and sunny, they decided to forego lunch at
an inn and to take a picnic with them. The party
was to consist of Anne and John Bellerman, Lord
Rayleigh, and Jane, all of whom were riding. At
the last minute the Marquis decided he wanted
the picnic lunch to be brought in the phaeton. He
asked David to drive.

The day started well. John Bellerman kept his
horse close to Jane's the whole way to Bury St.
Edmunds. To the secret delight of the whole
Heathfield staff, Anne's eldest brother was obviously smitten by Lady Jane. He followed her
around constantly, an expression in his eyes that
reminded David of a puppy dog he had once
owned. Jane was nice to him in an absent-minded
kind of way. She made polite conversation to him
now, even though she would have infinitely preferred to be riding behind with David.

The Marquis watched her surreptitiously. Her
obvious indifference worried him. It was not
natural for a girl her age to be so immune to the
charms of a handsome, personable, twenty-five-
year-old man who obviously adored her.

They dutifully toured the abbey and stopped
about halfway back to Heathfield to have their
picnic. David found them a pleasant glade and be-

gan to unload the phaeton as the others dismounted. The Marquis watched as John Bellerman
eagerly rushed to assist Jane to alight from her
sidesaddle. There was a suspicious quiver about
Jane's narrow, faultless nostrils as she allowed herself to be lifted to the ground. Wordlessly her eyes
flew to David, inviting him to share her amusement at Mr. Bellerman's unnecessary solicitude.
There was a faintly ironic look in David's amber
eyes as they met hers briefly, then they both
looked away, their faces identical masks of po-
liteness.

With a deep frown between his brows the Marquis helped Anne to dismount and moved forward to take charge of the picnic. After they had
all eaten, Jane suggested that Lord Rayleigh take
Anne and Mr. Bellerman to see a particularly fine
view that was about ten minutes' walk from where
they were.

"You must come too, Lady Jane," John Bellerman urged.

She shook her head. "I want to stay here with
David," she said bluntly.

"Then I shall remain also," he responded, moving toward where she was sitting on a rug.

Jane's eyes flashed blue sparks. "I am not going
to run away, Mr. Bellerman," she said, temper in
the crisp tones of her voice. "Go with Uncle Edward and your sister. You can see me when you
return."

Lord Rayleigh looked at his niece. "Come
along, John," he said genially. "Jane needs a rest."

Unwilling, but unable to refuse, Mr. Bellerman trailed sadly off after Lord Rayleigh and Anne. "Honestly!" Jane exploded when they were out of earshot. "He is driving me mad."

David just laughed. He dropped down beside her and stretched his length comfortably on the rug, leaning up on one elbow. He reached for a stalk of grass and began absently to chew it. A lock of sun-bright hair had fallen forward, half hiding his face. "How's the picture coming?" he asked.

Jane was painting a picture of Heathfield to give to Lord Rayleigh as a wedding present. It was a secret; only David knew about it. With a comfortable sigh she wrapped her arms around her updrawn knees and proceded to tell him about it.

The Marquis and his party were back much too quickly, she thought impatiently as she heard the sound of voices coming nearer. She shot a look at David from under her lashes and swore. He did not reply but, nearly imperceptibly, he smiled at her.

Lord Rayleigh had taken Mr. Bellerman with him because he recognized in Jane's face and voice the signs of an impending explosion. However, he had no intention of staying away for any length of time and, as his feelings were shared by both brother and sister, they soon retraced their steps to the glade. Anne and her brother went first and Lord Rayleigh kept his eyes on Mr. Bellerman as they returned. He was handsome, well-born, and

well-mannered, the sort of eligible man most
young girls dreamed about. What was the matter
with Jane, her uncle thought. He was beginning
to be afraid that Anne had been right about
David.

As they came into the clearing David rose to his
feet, holding a hand out to Jane with the ease of
long familiarity. To the Marquis's newly opened
eyes the unspoken intimacy that ran between the
girl and boy was startlingly apparent. It had taken
Anne, an outsider, to see what had eluded everyone else. He had wanted David to join their
outing so that Jane could contrast John Bellerman, socially acceptable and socially adept, to
David, whose role today had resembled that of a
servant. But Anne had been right; David was too
clearly a gentleman for him ever to appear as anything else. And, as he watched David's tall figure
effortlessly packing the phaeton, the Marquis
thought somewhat grimly that Anne had been
right about something else. It was now quite clear
to him why Jane was so maddeningly indifferent
to young Mr. Bellerman. To someone who was
used to looking at David, John Bellerman was
very insignificant indeed.

Chapter XI

And in this state she gallops night by night
Through lovers' brains, and then they dream of
love. . . .
—William Shakespeare

The Bellermans left Heathfield to return to Bedfordshire to prepare for the wedding. On the surface the household at Heathfield returned to its normal serenity, but beneath the surface there were hidden currents of stress.

David was finding it increasingly difficult to act naturally with Jane. Anne had mentioned to him that she planned to take Jane to London for the coming Season, and David knew what that meant. He had listened to too much gossip at race meets not to know that girls went to London to find husbands. Jane, he was quite sure, had no idea of getting married, but her uncle evidently was thinking ahead.

David knew, in his bones, that Jane would be miserable married to anyone but himself. But they would never let her marry him. Nor was she ready to talk about marriage; she was still too much a child.

Since there was nothing he could honorably say

to her, David said nothing. But he agonized that she would allow herself to be married off without realizing the implications of what marriage meant. And the thought of a future without her appalled him: a vista of empty, meaningless years stretching away in an endless road to nowhere.

Jane knew there was something bothering David, but she could not get out of him what it was. He would catch her looking at him with a worried, puzzled frown between her brows that made him want to grab her in his arms and kiss it away. She jokingly mentioned John Bellerman a few times; obviously she thought his devotion was ridiculous. It clearly had never occurred to her that young men *did* feel that way about young women and there would be many more men who would feel that way about herself. David found her denseness alternatingly endearing and exasperating. After all, he kept telling himself, she wouldn't be seventeen until next month.

Lord Rayleigh was also uneasy about a relationship he had for too long taken for granted. By the time he and Jane left for Bellerman Hall he had pretty well fathomed the state of David's feelings. He had mentioned to Jane, casually, that he expected her to come to London for a visit in the spring. As he had dwelled mainly on the opportunities she would have to see the great art collections of the capital, she had not protested loudly. When the subject came up within David's hearing, however, Lord Rayleigh had seen the sudden rigidity of the boy's back which, along with the spasmodic clenching of his lean hands, had given him away.

There was one other occasion when David's private emotions, usually kept well in check, were revealed to the observing Marquis. They were out on the heath one morning with five of the horses. Jane was galloping one of the mares while Lord Rayleigh, David, and the two grooms stood lined up to watch. She had lost her ribbon and as she galloped by her hair streamed out behind her like a black silk flag. She pulled the horse up and came toward them, her face brilliant with pleasure, and the Marquis turned momentarily to say something to David. What he saw in that still face struck him to the heart; an underlying desolation that spoke of an emotion that was intensely serious.

Lord Rayleigh was an innately good-hearted man. He liked David. But he could not allow his niece, Lady Jane Fitzmaurice, well-born, beautiful, and an heiress, to become involved with a boy who worked in his stables. Jane, who, thank God, was clear as water, obviously had no inkling of David's feelings. The Marquis was profoundly grateful that David had had the sense not to say anything to her. He did not want to have to fire the boy. And he would get Jane away to London as quickly as possible. He made a great effort to banish from his mind the look he had seen on David's face.

The union of Edward St. John Francis Stanton,

Marquis of Rayleigh, to Miss Anne Bellerman of Bellerman Hall was celebrated at the end of October with all due pomp and circumstance. Jane was a bridesmaid and performed her part in the ceremony with suitable gravity. The wedding took place in the chapel at Bellerman Hall and was attended by large numbers of the bride's family. The groom's family consisted of his niece and numerous cousins and friends.

Jane was delighted to see Lord Massingham, Mr. Firth, and Sir Henry Graham, all of whom she knew well. She hated strangers and immediately joined one or the other of them whenever she got a chance. For their part, Lord Rayleigh's friends, all confirmed bachelors, were pleased with her company. They were all horse-mad and consequently had always approved of Jane. Nor were they blind to her beauty. The four of them had a much better time at the wedding than they had expected to. Their enjoyment was not looked on kindly by Lady Bellerman, who disapproved of Jane's obvious intimacy with such famous Corinthians.

After the wedding party had departed, Jane found herself the only guest at Bellerman Hall. John Bellerman, at the request of Lord Rayleigh, was shooting with friends in Scotland. The Marquis had no desire to encourage young Mr. Bellerman's unreciprocated infatuation. He had concluded that it would take a very different kind of man to attract Jane.

Bellerman Hall was quiet, but Jane was not

idle. She had brought two of her hunters with her and was out practically every day with the local pack. She soon became friendly with Sir Thomas Osborne, the local squire, who was fifty-five, bluff, vulgar, amiable, and hunting-mad. He had not been pleased to have Jane join his hunt, but after the first day he became her devoted slave. They spent hours in the office of Sir Thomas's stables, discussing various aspects of hunting and exchanging stories.

Lady Bellerman was scandalized. Jane's riding outfit was her first sin. Instead of the full-skirted, floor-length habits women commonly wore, Jane appeared in an ankle-length divided skirt of heavy melton cloth with a tailored jacket and a man's hat. The dreadfulness of this apparel was almost forgotten, however, when Lady Bellerman learned that Jane rode astride. Jane's reassurances that her uncle perfectly approved did little to soothe Lady Bellerman's outraged feelings.

Then Lady Bellerman learned that Jane was rapidly becoming the bosom friend of Sir Thomas Osborne. Lady Bellerman vehemently disapproved of the Squire. She thought him crude, rude, and boorish. When she pointed out all his faults to Jane, her maddening guest merely replied that Sir Thomas was a first-class hunting man. As if, Lady Bellerman thought in exasperation, that had anything to do with his suitability as a companion for a seventeen-year-old girl.

All these disputes, however, were merely preliminary skirmishes. The real battle came after

Jane had been two weeks at Bellerman Hall. On that memorable day she returned from the hunting field to be greeted by the butler, who requested her to attend Lady Bellerman in the blue saloon. Without bothering to change, Jane went down the hall, wondering what grave offense she was guilty of this time. Jane had been very polite to Lady Bellerman thus far. She had listened respectfully to all her hostess's strictures before proceeding to do exactly as she chose.

She found both Lord and Lady Bellerman in the blue saloon, taking tea. Lady Bellerman looked exceedingly grave. "This letter arrived for you in today's post, Jane," she said, picking up a letter from the side table.

Jane's extraordinary eyes lit. "Oh, good. My letter from David. May I have it, please?"

"I thought perhaps that was who it was from," Lady Bellerman said even more gravely than before. She had heard something of David from both her son and her daughter. She agreed with them that it was not a relationship that should be encouraged. "I do not think I can give you this letter, Jane," she said unwisely.

Jane was very still. "What do you mean?" Her voice was ominously quiet.

"You should not be allowed to correspond with this stableboy. You are not a child any longer, and I feel it is my duty, while you are under my care, to censor your mail as if you were my own daughter. Your uncle is an excellent man, but gentlemen are never the best judge of what is good for a

young girl. You must allow me to decide matters
of this kind for you."

Jane listened to this magisterial speech in an astonished silence. Then her eyes narrowed danger-
ously and her voice, when she spoke, was so cold,
so exact, that it virtually paralysed her listeners.
"Whom do you think you are speaking to?" she
asked Lady Bellerman, her eyes like blue ice. "I
have been extremely forebearing with you, Lady
Bellerman, but I will not tolerate this kind of in-
terference. I must inform you that I am not accustomed to having my clothing, my behavior, and
my friends criticized by persons whom I scarcely
know. The only person with a right to criticize
what I choose to do and whom I choose to know is
my uncle. Now either you give me my letter or I
leave Bellerman Hall. Immediately."

There was a catastrophic silence as Lady Bellerman stared at the beautiful, implacable face of
her young guest. Very slowly she held out David's
letter. Jane took it. "Thank you," she said curtly,
and turning on her heel, left the room.

Lady Bellerman turned to her husband. "Well!"
she ejaculated weakly.

There was a gleam of admiration in his eyes.
"She was right, Lizzie," he told his outraged
spouse. "You overstepped yourself. What's more,
you'd better leave the girl alone or she'll carry out
her threat and bolt back to Heathfield. Rayleigh
won't relish the scandal if she does that."

"She is a termagant," Lady Bellerman said, her

voice gaining strength. "I pity poor Anne from the bottom of my heart."

"They'll probably get along just fine," Lord Bellerman prophesied. "Anne won't make the mistake of crossing her like you just did. Let her uncle keep her in line. If he can."

Chapter XII

Seems, madam! nay, it is; I know not "seems."
  —William Shakespeare

Lord and Lady Rayleigh collected Jane from Bellerman Hall in early December and they all returned to Newmarket for the holidays. Christmas was usually a busy time at Heathfield. There was always a house party of the Marquis's friends, which entailed daily hunting and shooting expeditions. Anne had been a trifle apprehensive about taking over from Jane the role of hostess and chatelaine of Heathfield. She need not have worried; it was a role Jane had never had much interest in playing. Anne had an inkling of this when Jane blithely referred her to Mrs. Andrews, the housekeeper, who "saw to all that sort of thing."

Jane did, in fact, consult with the cook and kitchen staff daily, but the purpose of her visits was not to discuss the day's menu but to sample something from the pantry. Anne was startled, when she arrived in the kitchen one morning to inspect her new domain, to find Jane lounging at the big wooden table chewing on a pastry and chatting in flawless French with Alphonse, the Marquis's august chef. They were arguing amia-

bly about the virtues of democracy. Jane was for
it; Alphonse definitely was not.

Anne had been very strictly reared by Lady Bellerman and was somewhat shocked to discover her
husband's niece to be on such terms of intimacy
with the servants. When she found out that Jane
also played cards, for money, with the grooms, she
broke her own unwritten rule and mentioned
Jane's behavior, not to Lord Rayleigh this time,
but to Jane herself.

She had scarcely got started on her tentative lecture before Jane interrupted her. "Poor Anne,"
she said sympathetically. "I suppose you can't help
being such a slave to convention. Your mother
probably nursed you on it."

"I beg your pardon," Anne said faintly.

"She tried it on me, too," Jane said scornfully,
"but I soon put a halt to her."

Anne stared at Jane wonderingly. To her
knowledge, no one had ever successfully "put a
halt to" her mother. "I may be a slave to convention, as you say, Jane," she responded finally, "but
there are certain things a lady just does not do.
She does not, for example, hobnob with the servants."

"Why not?" Jane asked flatly.

"It undermines discipline," Anne said. "It is
never wise to encourage vulgar persons——"

Jane cut in, "The servants at Heathfield are not
vulgar. Many of them have excellent understand-
ings. I like them. I have no intention of ceasing to
'hobnob' with them. It is vulgar, Anne, to allow

other people's opinions to divert you from what you know is right. It is vulgar and cowardly and unintelligent. Great heavens, Anne," she concluded, and centuries of untarnished pride sounded in her voice, "I am Jane Fitzmaurice. What do I care what a pack of gossiping old women like your mother think of me?"

Jane was obviously sincere. She was Jane Fitzmaurice and did what she liked. Anne felt a pang of envy; it must be marvelous to be so self-confident, she thought. "I don't know what to say to you, Jane," she answered finally. "I have always been taught to be mindful of the feelings of others."

"I am mindful of the feelings of those people I care about," Jane returned.

"What if David asked you to stop doing something because he didn't like it?" Anne queried slowly, conscious of treading on dangerous ground.

"I would stop doing it," Jane answered promptly.

"Why?"

The answer came just as readily. "Because David is intelligent. He has reasons for what he says and does. He understands people much better than I do."

Anne raised her eyebrows faintly. "And I, I take it, am not intelligent?"

Jane looked impatient. "That's not fair, Anne. You appear to be perfectly sensible, but your mother is not. And when you parrot your mother, you really cannot expect me to pay much attention. It's too absurd." Jane headed for the door feeling she had had enough of this conversation. "The next thing I know, you'll be trying to tell me I mustn't know David!" she said, a parting shot to demonstrate the idiocy of Anne's whole point of view.

The Christmas houseparty went on for longer than usual this year, to be followed by a series of other parties arranged by the Marquis. Jane was kept very busy, which was the main purpose of such continuous entertaining by Lord and Lady Rayleigh.

"I hardly get a chance to see you anymore," Jane complained to David one morning when she had come down to the stables before breakfast purposely to seek him out. "It is like a hotel up at the house. We run one group in, mount them on horses, send them out with guns, feed them, bed them, send them on their way, and before the last of them is down the drive, the new group is arriving. Is it always like this in the winter?"

"It has never been as busy as this," David told her. "I expect Lord Rayleigh wants to introduce his wife to all his friends."

"Well, I don't see why they can't go visit someone else's house for a change," Jane grumbled. "Then perhaps you and I could have a moment's peace together."

Peace was something that David was finding impossible to achieve. He had a good idea of Lord

Rayleigh's motives in filling his house with company. David had not missed the anxious glances the Marquis occasionally cast toward himself and Jane whenever they chanced to be together. And David himself hardly knew what he dreaded more: to be with her and have to dissemble or to be without her. Either option was unbearably bleak.

It was almost with relief that David learned they were leaving for London. It was March and the Season wouldn't really get started for another month, but the Marquis was anxious to remove Jane from Heathfield and David, and Anne said it would take some time to provide Jane with a proper wardrobe. They told Jane they would return to Heathfield for the first Newmarket Meet and Jane assumed that she would remain at home for the rest of the summer. They did not disabuse her of her notion.

Jane's main impression of London during the first week of their residence there was that it was filled with shops. Anne insisted on buying her a whole wardrobe from the inside out. "You will be accompanying me to parties, Jane, and you must look presentable," she said when Jane balked.

Jane was not at all interested in going to parties, but she was willing to humor Anne a little. "I can see the need for a few new dresses," she said reasonably, "but you are getting carried away, Anne. How many parties do you expect to attend, for heaven's sake?"

"Many," Anne said firmly, and steered her into yet another shop.

At first Jane had not minded greatly. Her artist's eye appreciated the beauty of the colors and fabrics of the frocks she tried on. And Anne was relieved to discover that Jane's taste was impeccable. After a week, however, she rebelled. There was a heated argument between the two girls which left them both exasperated and feeling the other one was totally unreasonable.

"I never heard of a girl who didn't want new clothes!" Anne finally cried.

"Anne, if you mention one more word about clothes," Jane said with dangerous calm, "I will take a scissor to the mountains of garments you have already purchased for me." She meant it. Anne capitulated.

"Very well, I suppose I can finish the shopping myself. There are only gloves and shawls and things like that left to purchase."

"Splendid. You do that," Jane told her.

"And what are you so anxious to do, Jane," Anne asked stiffly, "that you can't take time to shop with me?"

Jane's eyes sparkled. "I am going to look at paintings," she said with great satisfaction.

The first letter David received from Jane in London had been full of complaints about shopping. The second was quite different.

"Dear David," it began. "I have made the acquaintance of the most marvelous painter. His name is Mr. Turner and he has a studio here in London. I was looking for a painting to send as a present to Miss Becker, and my uncle took me to the Royal Academy. It was there that I saw Mr. Turner's work for the first time.

"David, he is magnificent. Next day I dragged Anne around to his studio in Harley Street and saw some more of his work. He had two things in particular—one a picture of the falls at Schaffhausen and another of a shipwreck—that were the most wonderful things I have ever seen. I dream about them. The color! The light!

"He is very shy, but he was terribly kind to me. He invited me to attend a lecture he is giving on perspective at the Royal Academy and he asked to see a sample of my work. I'm extremely nervous. This is a man whose opinion I would tremble before. What if he doesn't like what I am doing?

"I am to see him again in two days' time. I shall write to tell you what happens. It hangs over me like the Day of Judgment.

"But enough of me and my doings. How are you? How do things look for the Newmarket Meet?"

The rest of the letter dealt with David, Heathfield, and the horses. Only one paragraph at the end of this rather lengthy epistle referred to the social world of London, to which she was to be formally introduced in a week's time. "Uncle Edward is throwing a big ball next week," she wrote. "Anne is in a frenzy over it. They have invited five hundred people! It is going to be dreadful.

Imagine the boredom of an evening spent trying to be polite to five hundred strangers. However, Anne and Uncle Edward seem to think I should be overjoyed at the prospect, so I dutifully smile whenever they bring the subject up. The only thing that has interested me so far, I must honestly say, is the food. There are going to be lobster patties. I think I shall spend the evening in the supper room."

Thus wrote Jane on the eve of her debut at the first and the most brilliant ball of the London Season.

Chapter XIII

O, she doth teach the torches to burn bright!
—William Shakespeare

Rayleigh House in Grosvenor Square was brilliantly lit on the night of the ball given by the Marquis and Marchioness of Rayleigh to introduce the Marquis's niece, Lady Jane Fitzmaurice, to London Society. Carriages were lined up before the house, waiting for up to forty-five minutes before it was their turn to pull up before the door of Rayleigh House. The marble hall was filled with the most distinguished persons in town, all talking and laughing as they waited to go up the stairs to greet their host and hostess.

The ball was a success before it even started. All of the Right People had come. Many of them came because of the Marquis; quite a few came because of Anne; all came because they were intensely curious to meet Jane. The rumor of her beauty combined with some hair-raising tales about her exploits on the hunting field had piqued the curiosity of the ton. They were not disappointed.

Jane wore a dress of palest ice blue gauze over an underdress of white satin. Her hair was dressed high over a pearl-encrusted comb. Around her slender neck were clasped her mother's pearls. Her eyes, the color of which was repeated in her gown, were startling against the black of her hair and lashes. She smiled rarely; there was a look of beautiful severity on her face as she stood beside Anne, greeting the arriving guests.

Long before the last of the guests had arrived, Jane's hand had been claimed for every dance. Anne had told her not to dance twice with anyone and Jane had no pangs about following her instructions. She moved through the evening unaware of the effect her beauty and the strange intensity of her personality were having upon her partners. No one before had ever seen such a self-possessed seventeen-year-old debutante. Her manners were impeccable, but the arrogant carriage of her head betrayed her. Jane was not impressed by London Society.

John Bellerman had asked her to have supper with him and Jane had been happy to accept. John Bellerman at Heathfield had been a nuisance; in London, he was a familiar face and Jane, who was only comfortable among people she knew, was genuinely glad to see him.

"There are lobster patties," she told him seriously. "Let's make sure we get there before they are all gone."

He was happy to oblige. He found her a seat and had gone off to fill up some plates when Anne came up to her with a tall, fair man. "Jane," she said, "may I introduce Mr. Julian Wrexham? If you don't mind, we will join you and John for supper."

Jane looked up into the handsome, fine-boned face of Julian Wrexham and felt a slight shock of recognition. She frowned slightly as she acknowledged the introduction and turned to Anne after he had gone to procure her some supper. "Who is Mr. Wrexham, Anne?" she asked. "He looks familiar. Have I ever met him?"

"I don't think so, Jane," Anne answered. "He is not part of your uncle's set."

"Oh. Then he is a friend of yours."

"Not really, although I am of course acquainted with him."

Jane stared at her in amazement. "If neither you nor Uncle Edward knows him, why on earth did you invite him?"

Anne sighed. "Jane, you are such an innocent. Wrexham is the nephew and heir of the Earl of Wymondham, one of the premier noblemen in the kingdom. As such, he is asked everywhere. I am delighted that he chose to accept our invitation." What she did not say was that Wrexham was *the* prime catch on London's marriage mart. He was twenty-eight, heir to one of the greatest and richest earldoms in England, and so far had proved to be very elusive. He had raised expectations in the hearts of many young ladies and their mamas, but none had brought him up to scratch so far. He had taken one look at Jane and demanded to be introduced. When Anne had regretfully told him that Jane was engaged for every dance, he had suggested that they join her for supper. Anne had been more than happy to oblige him. If Jane could attach Wrexham!

Anne came out of her pleasant dream to hear Jane speaking to her. "I beg your pardon, Jane?" she said.

Jane raised an eyebrow but patiently repeated her question. "I asked you if Lord Wymondham was a bachelor? You said Mr. Wrexham was his nephew."

"Lord Wymondham is married, but has never had children. His wife does not care for the English climate and lives in Italy. Wymondham himself rarely comes to London. He is often engaged in diplomatic missions which take him all over the world."

"He and his wife don't get along, I gather," Jane said cynically.

"No, they don't." Anne hesitated, then ventured her first hint about their real purpose in bringing Jane to London. "I believe the Earl was married very young, in France. The Wrexhams did not approve and he was brought home. His wife was killed in the revolution. There was a child, too, I believe. Anyway, a few years later he married Annabella Stackley, a former actress. He did it to spite his family, I believe, but he ended up spiting himself. They never got on." Anne paused, then said delicately, "Your uncle would never force you to marry someone you did not like, Jane. But it is very important when one marries to choose someone with whom one is compatible, both in temperament and in class."

Jane looked startled. "Married! Good heavens, Anne, who said anything about my getting married?"

At this John returned, not overly pleased to see that his sister had intruded on his tête à tête. When he saw Mr. Wrexham his temper deteriorated even further. If Julian Wrexham was going to dangle after Jane, the rest of her admirers might as well fold their tents and retire from the field.

To her surprise, Jane found that she was enjoying her visit to London. It was not the avalanche of invitations that poured into the house or the admiration of many of London's most distinguished bachelors that impressed her. It was the art.

There were as yet no public galleries in London, but aside from the Royal Academy, artists' studios, and the art sale rooms, Jane was able to see a great many private collections. A number of rich English connoisseurs had been able to buy up masterpieces from the great collections in France, Italy, and Spain that had been broken up after the French Revolution. Consequently, there was a fund of European masterpieces gracing the walls of English houses. Mr. Morely, nephew of the Duke of Melrose, took Jane to see his uncle's collection of seventeenth-century Dutch landscapes. Lord Henry Markham, son of the Earl of Newcastle, took her on a tour of his father's famous

Titian gallery. Sir George Beaumont not only showed her his great collection of Italian and French masters, he loaned her a Raphael to take home and study at her leisure.

Julian Wrexham was also well known for his appreciation and understanding of art, and the Wymondham collection, to which he was heir, was justly famous. One afternoon about a week after the Rayleigh Ball, he invited Jane and Anne to visit Hawkhurst House, the London home of the Earls of Wymondham. The house was outside the city proper, set in a lovely park that stretched down to the Thames. It was an Elizabethan mansion that the father of the present Earl had had redone by Robert Adam. It was used as a country house convenient to town and it was famous as one of Adam's most brilliant interiors.

"My uncle uses it whenever he is in town, which is but seldom, I might say," Mr. Wrexham told them. "I stay here occasionally myself, but I often find my bachelor's lodgings in town more convenient. I have had as yet no need for a larger establishment." His gray eyes had looked speculatively at Jane, who was staring at the building in front of them and appeared unconscious of his regard. Anne was very aware of that look, however, and felt a faint thrill run up her spine. She felt Mr. Wrexham's gaze move to her face and hastily focused her own eyes on the façade of Hawkhurst House.

It was a great quadrangular mansion that dated from the sixteenth century and the Elizabethan exterior had remained largely untouched. The four wings of the building were built around a courtyard and the north side, where they were entering, contained the state rooms which Adam had decorated so ambitiously.

They started in the entrance hall, filled with marbles set in classical arches, and worked their way slowly through the anteroom and dining room. Mr. Wrexham led them from one fine thing to another, discoursing lightly and knowledgeably about each piece, consulting their own opinions with flattering attention. After a while, Anne found herself becoming oppressed by such an accumulation of beauty and knowledge, but she continued to look attentively at Julian Wrexham and to smile and admire politely. Jane was more silent. It was not until they reached the green drawing room that she became animated. The walls were lined with green silk and hung with paintings by Rembrandt, Rubens, and Claude. They spent quite a bit of time in the drawing room and Anne's legs were aching by the time they had made their way to the gallery where tea was to be served.

The long Elizabethan gallery had been done over by Adam into a delightful room for the ladies to retire to after a formal dinner party. On the walls hung a collection of Suffolk scenes by Constable. "My uncle added these," Mr. Wrexham told Jane somewhat apologetically. "Mr. Constable is not very well thought of among most of the great collectors, but my uncle likes his work."

"Your uncle is right," said Jane with decision. "I saw some of his paintings at the Royal Academy." She was silent a minute, looking quietly at the peaceful scene before her. "Look at the way the light and shade of the trees is reflected in the river there," she said finally. "Beautiful."

Wrexham looked from the painting to Jane's intent face. "Yes," he agreed pensively. "Beautiful."

On the whole Anne was well pleased with the afternoon. Julian Wrexham could not have been more charming, she thought. "It must be marvelous to live in a house like that," she said to Jane as they drove back to town together. "Especially for a man like Mr. Wrexham, who obviously has a deep love for beautiful things."

"I don't know if he does, really," said Jane thoughtfully. "I had the feeling all afternoon that he didn't so much want us to admire his house as he wanted us to admire *him* for owning it."

This was an uncomfortably perceptive comment. Anne, too, had had the impression that Julian Wrexham was in effect presenting his credentials to Jane. It was not a thought that made Anne at all unhappy. "He wants *you* to think well of him," she said finally. "After all, that is not such a bad thing."

"It shows a very shallow feeling about art," said Jane positively.

Anne sighed, leaned back in her seat, and closed her eyes.

Chapter XIV

"Is it a custom?"
—William Shakespeare

The weeks went by and Jane found herself locked
into a social whirl that made all her previous ex-
periences pale. She went to balls, receptions,
routs, luncheon parties, dinner parties, and to Almacks, London's most exclusive social club, known
irreverently as the marriage mart. There was a
solid core of bachelors who spent a great deal of
time dancing with her, driving her in the park,
and fetching her glasses of punch. Jane did not
have the kind of personality that appealed to everyone. The more frivolous members of the dandy
set melted away before the scornful look in her
eyes, and there were some who found her obvious
boredom with most of London's famous Season
rather daunting. But several of the town's most
desirable men were very interested in this slight,
proud young girl with the extraordinary blue-
green eyes.

Jane, to the intense irritation of her uncle, developed a definite partiality for the company of
the Earl of Bocking. They shared an interest in
horses; the Earl did not have a racing stable of his

own, but he spent many hours at Newmarket, Epsom, Cheltenham, and other race courses around the country. He was an inveterate gambler and delighted in picking Jane's brain about what horses she thought would be worth watching at upcoming meets.

Lord Bocking also was a great art collector. Jane had been invited to view his collection of Roman marbles and Italian masters. "A fellow I knew in Rome sent me all these things before Napoleon moved in," he told Jane. "What do you think of this da Vinci, eh?"

Lastly, they shared a similar sense of humor and a similar intolerance for the frantic pursuit of pleasure that was the chief hallmark of Regency society. "Most of these people," Jane said scornfully to Lord Bocking, "tinkle, they are so empty. Nothing matters to them except the cut of a coat or the way a neckcloth is tied. And the women are just as bad. Who danced with whom and how many times is all they worry about."

Lord Bocking was a great comfort to Jane, so she couldn't quite understand Anne's reasoning when she remonstrated with Jane for spending so much time with him. "He is perfectly respectable, Anne," she said in a genuinely puzzled voice. "I like him. Why shouldn't I spend time talking with him?"

"I agree with you that he is perfectly respectable, if a little odd," Anne responded. "But he is sixty-two years old, Jane! You sat out two dances at Lady Cowper's ball the other night talking to him. And you let him take you in to supper! What about all the *young* men who want to talk to you?"

"They aren't as interesting," Jane said simply, leaving Anne almost at the point of grinding her teeth.

The Marquis had thrown up his hands in despair when Anne related this conversation to him. "She is impossible," he said. "All of London—or at least an impressive part of it—is ready to fall at her feet and what does she do? She spends her time hobnobbing with an eccentric old man who could be her grandfather, for God's sake."

"She feels comfortable with him, Edward," said Anne. "She understands him. She does not understand many of the other people she has met. They live by a code that is foreign to her."

The Marquis rubbed a hand across his forehead. "You mean they enjoy parties and she does not." He looked at Anne somberly. "Jane is by nature the most unsociable being I have ever met. I've often thought it was my fault. After all, I was responsible for bringing her up. She was probably allowed to be too solitary as a child."

Anne had learned a great deal about Jane in the six months since her marriage. "It isn't your fault, Edward," she said firmly. "In fact, I think you were the best thing that ever happened to her. You gave her room to breathe. A conventional childhood would have driven her wild."

The Marquis frowned. "What is the matter with her, Anne? Why is she always so difficult?"

"I think, Edward, that Jane is an extraordinarily talented painter." Anne spoke slowly. "I told you that Mr. Turner was very impressed with her work. He has given her a great deal of time, and I understand that such interest on his part is quite unusual."

"Very few painters look like Jane," his lordship said cynically.

"That's not it," Anne replied seriously. "It is her work he is interested in."

"It is good," his lordship admitted. "That painting she did of the Heathfield stables is as good as anything I've ever seen."

Anne smiled at him affectionately. "You would think any painting of your precious horses was magnificent."

He grinned. "True."

"But to get back to Jane," she sighed. "She is beginning to rebel about going to all these parties. She hasn't time to work, she says."

"Every other young girl her age is working at getting a husband," he exploded. "I would have an artistic genius for a niece, who acts as if she never heard of the word."

"Now Edward," Anne said soothingly. "You know you love Jane. You would hate it if she changed."

"I'm not so sure about that," he said, his face grim. "I'd live a lot longer, that's for sure."

"Well, I wouldn't despair just yet. She seems to

like Mr. Wrexham. At any rate, she never looks
bored in his company, as she so regrettably does
with a great many other of her admirers."

The Marquis raised an eyebrow. "Wrexham,
eh? He has a reputation for being a difficult fish
to land, Anne."

"Jane is not fishing for *him*," said Anne primly.

"True. He might even find that intriguing." He
looked thoughtful. "You think she likes him?"

"Apparently. How much she likes him, Edward,
is quite another matter, though."

"I know." He brightened as a thought struck
him. "I haven't heard her mention David lately.
Surely that is a good sign." The Marquis had
shared his fears with Anne by now.

"One would think so," she replied in an expressionless tone. In fact, Jane's uncharacteristic
reticence about David made her anxious, but she
did not want to worry the Marquis.

He mistook her tone. "I'm sorry, love. I didn't
mean to tire you out." Anne was pregnant and
feeling it occasionally.

She smiled at him, pleased by the concern in his
eyes. "You haven't tired me, my lord," she answered softly.

"Is Jane too much for you? If she is, just say the
word and I'll send her home." A rueful smile
crossed his face. "She'll be only too happy to go."

"Nonsense," Anne said with a briskness that was
contradicted by the tenderness of her mouth. "I
am perfectly fine. You are not to worry about
me."

He bent to kiss the top of her head. "All right, but let me know if it becomes too much for you. If it does, we can all go home to Heathfield together."

"I hope when we do Jane will be suitably engaged," said Anne. "We all go to Carlton House tomorrow night for Prinny's reception. Julian Wrexham will be there. Perhaps you could talk to him, Edward, and try to fathom what his feelings are."

"All right," the Marquis said gloomily, "but I know what Jane will be doing."

Anne laughed. "Of course. She will be looking at the pictures."

Jane was indeed anxious to see Carlton House. The Prince of Wales had refurbished it at enormous expense and it held one of the greatest art collections in Britain. Prinny, as the Prince was called, although not to his face, held no great interest for Jane. She had seen him numerous times at Newmarket, although she had always been too young to be presented to him.

There was a large gathering of people at Carlton House. The Marquis, who did not often frequent governmental circles, was a little perplexed as to why he had been invited on this particular occasion. The rooms were filled with cabinet ministers and ambassadors. His puzzlement cleared, however, when the Prince himself came over to speak to him. "My dear Rayleigh," said His Royal Highness with all the charm for which he was so justly famous. "I am so glad to see you. You must present your niece to me. I have heard a great deal about her." He turned to Jane, who was looking as demure as it was possible for her in a dress of white gauze.

The Marquis presented her and she sank into a graceful curtsy. "I have heard you are an art lover, Lady Jane," said the Prince jovially. "You must let me show you my collection."

Jane did not appear to be at all overcome by this honor. Her eyes, candid and brilliant, met his directly. "I should love that, Your Highness," she said sincerely and, taking the arm he offered, let him walk her off.

The Marquis turned to find his wife had arrived back at his side accompanied by Julian Wrexham. "I'm not sure I like this," Anne said a trifle uneasily. "You know what his reputation is."

The Marquis looked amused. "I shouldn't be concerned, my dear. Jane isn't at all his type. She's much too young. And I have every confidence in her ability to control his—er—wayward passions."

Anne need not have worried. Jane and the Prince of Wales were getting along famously, but amour was very far from their minds. The Prince knew quite a lot about the art he had collected and Jane listened to him intently, occasionally asking a pertinent question. They were very pleased with each other when they returned to the main reception room, where they were immediately joined by a group of men who included the Home Secretary and the First Lord of the

Treasury. They stood gathered together in front of the marble fireplace, talking and laughing, and the Prince made no move to return Jane to her aunt and uncle. In fact, she appeared to be the center of the conversation.

"I hope she is not telling them about her admiration for pure democracy," murmured the Marquis.

"Does Lady Jane favor democracy?" asked Mr. Wrexham coolly.

"I'm afraid so. She is very fond of Rousseau, at any rate."

"She sounds well educated."

The Marquis laughed. "You wouldn't say that if you'd seen the way she cheated on her Latin translations."

Mr. Wrexham turned to stare at Jane's uncle. "Latin?" he said incredulously.

"Latin," the Marquis said mournfully. "Jane never does anything else other young girls do, so why should her education be like theirs? She studied Latin."

"I see." Wrexham's eyes were on the slight black and white figure so effortlessly dominating the scene by the fireplace and his face was inscrutable. "Lady Jane is, as you say, unique," he murmured. But whether or not he meant it as a compliment was something the Marquis could not decide.

Chapter XV

Tell me daughter Juliet,
How stands your disposition to be married?
—William Shakespeare

Julian Wrexham was a connoisseur of fine things and in Jane he recognized the quality of wife he was looking for. He was not a man to be satisfied by the usual; he wanted a woman of beauty and birth, of course, but she must have a distinction beyond that. There was a look of flawless pride about Jane that had attracted him from the first. It was the right look for the future Countess of Wymondham. Jane would suit a great role in society, which always admired an air of superiority. And she would be a fitting complement to the beauties of Hawkhurst House and Wymondham. The more Mr. Wrexham thought about it, the more he became convinced that this would be the kind of marriage suitable to his cultivated aestheticism.

"The betting in the club is heavily in favor of your making Lady Jane Fitzmaurice an offer before the end of the summer," Wrexham's friend

Mr. Court said one afternoon as they shot billiards at White's.

Julian Wrexham looked up. "Where does your money lie, my dear Court?" he asked pleasantly.

"Oh, you'll make her an offer," his friend replied. "She is the only girl you have ever seen who was not dying to marry you. The temptation must be irresistible."

Wrexham lined up a shot and made it. "It is, rather," he murmured.

Mr. Court shook his head ruefully. "She's a beauty, I grant you, but she'll make you a damn uncomfortable wife, Wrexham. Too independent. You'll never be able to count on her doing the expected thing."

Julian Wrexham looked amused. His egotism had never taken the crude form of desiring a dull wife. "Lady Jane has the distinction of being intelligent," he said. "It is a quality rare among the young ladies I have met."

"It is not just that," Mr. Court said soberly and with some insight. "Most girls are brought up to think that a woman's first duty is to please a man. The little Fitzmaurice doesn't think that at all. She had intentions of her own quite apart from any of us. One gets the impression she feels she is meant for more than a woman's usual lot in life. It is what makes her so interesting, but one has to question how desirable that quality would be in one's wife."

Wrexham smiled. "I don't pretend to know what other people are 'meant for,' Court. I only

know what I can do with them. Lady Jane is the
sort of wife who will suit me. She does what no
other woman has ever done; she satisfies the imagination."

Mr. Court looked somewhat dubiously at his
friend. "She's not a piece of art, Wrexham." There
was a small silence, then he said, "Well, don't ever
say I didn't warn you."

"I take due notice of your warning, my dear
Court," Wrexham replied gently. "I take due notice."

The next day Julian Wrexham called at
Grosvenor Square to see if Jane wanted to go driving with him. He found only Anne at home; Jane
and the Marquis had gone to a luncheon party at
Lady Carisbrook's. Civilly, Mr. Wrexham sat
down to talk a few minutes with Anne and while
he was there Jane and the Marquis returned.

They came into the room, both faces alight with
laughter. "How do you do, Mr. Wrexham?" Jane
said, sinking gracefully into a gold wing chair.
Her voice was breathless with mirth.

"What is so funny?" Anne asked, looking inquir-
ingly at her husband's flushed face.

The Marquis, an uncertain tremor in his voice,
began to relate the tale of the luncheon party. It
involved a drunken butler, a spastic footman, and
Lady Jersey as chief guest. In the middle of Lord
Rayleigh's recital, Jane leaped up and began to
act out the tableau, all the while keeping up a
mercilessly accurate mimicry of Lady Jersey's

monologue as catastrophe succeeded catastrophe. Her audience was crying with laughter by the time she had finished.

"Oh Lord," Mr. Wrexham said when he had gotten his voice back. "How I wish I'd been there."

"It was the best party I've been to in London," said Jane. "When I think of how Lady Carisbrook looked. . . ."

"Don't, Jane," Lord Rayleigh begged. "I can't stand it."

Anne wiped streaming eyes. "Poor Sophia Carisbrook. She will never live it down."

"Well I, for one, shall make a point of attending every party she invites me to." Jane rose. "If you will excuse me now. . . ."

"Jane," Anne said hurriedly, "Mr. Wrexham came to ask you to go driving with him."

"Thank you very much, Mr. Wrexham," Jane said absently, "but I have some work to do. The light is just about right now. Some other time, perhaps." She smiled graciously at the three of them and left the room with her swift, graceful stride.

Anne sighed. "I am sorry, Mr. Wrexham," she began, but he forestalled her.

"Please do not apologize, Lady Rayleigh. I only came on the chance Lady Jane would be free." He turned to the Marquis. "Since I am not to go driving, I wonder if I might have a word with you, Lord Rayleigh?"

"Certainly." The Marquis rose courteously.

"Let us go to the library." As the tall, elegant figure of Julian Wrexham passed out of the room, the Marquis exchanged a meaningful glance with his wife.

He was back in less than half an hour. He closed the door behind him and stood regarding her gravely. "He wants to marry Jane," he said.

Anne clasped her hands tightly. "Oh, Edward."

"I told him he had my permission to speak to her. He is coming back tomorrow morning."

Anne wet her lips. "He is the catch of the year. Do you think she'll accept him, Edward?"

"I don't know." There was a pause, then he said slowly, "I am not going to say anything to her, Anne. Let Wrexham handle it. He'll do a better job of pleading for himself than I ever could. And she does seem to like him." He looked at her questioningly and she nodded in response. She knew the last thing the Marquis wanted to do was to face Jane on this subject.

"That will be best," she said placidly.

He walked across the room and sat down beside her. "If anyone can get her to the altar, he is the man," he said somewhat hollowly. Anne smiled reassuringly up at him and he picked up her hand and kissed it. "Thank God for you, Anne," he said fervently. "You are so *restful*."

Mr. Wrexham returned the next morning as promised and Anne summoned Jane to the drawing room. Then she made an excuse and left them alone together in the large, silk-hung room.

Jane looked faintly startled and Mr. Wrexham crossed the room to stand before her. His hair shone silver in the light from the candles, lit against the dark, rainy day, and there was a look of tenderness in his eyes that she had not seen there before. "Don't look so bewildered, Lady Jane," he said gently. "I hope you won't be angry, but I asked Lady Rayleigh for this opportunity to speak to you privately."

"Oh," said Jane. She was looking at him warily, as a wild creature might look when it is finally cornered.

"Yes." He looked at her for a moment and then said simply, "What I wish to say to you is that I find I'm in love with you."

"You musn't say that." Her hands were clasped tightly together in front of her.

"I realize that I had no right to speak to you before now," he agreed gravely. "But your uncle gave me permission yesterday to address you."

Jane was very still. "Uncle Edward said you might marry me?" Her voice was toneless.

"He said I might ask you," he corrected her gently. He took her cold hands into his and spoke persuasively, "I love you very much indeed, Lady Jane. You are the only woman in the world for me. If you should consent to be my wife, you would make me the happiest of men."

Jane's nostrils had stiffened, but otherwise her face had not changed. "I must confess you have taken me by surprise, Mr. Wrexham. I have not thought much about marriage. I am only seventeen, you know."

"And I am twenty-eight. There is a very reasonable age difference between us; and many girls are married at seventeen."

She looked up directly into his eyes, an odd, untouched reserve in her own. "But I don't know you very well."

He smiled. "That can be remedied."

"Yes, I suppose it can." She transferred her gaze to the top button of his coat and removed her hands from his. "I am, of course, honored that you should make me this offer, Mr. Wrexham," she said finally in a stilted voice. "However, I do not feel prepared to give you an answer at present."

A slight frown appeared between his fair brows. "I see." There was a short silence, then he said with an anxiety that he made no attempt to conceal, "I hope you are not telling me I may not think of you."

"No, Mr. Wrexham," Jane replied steadily. "I am saying that I should like to know you better before I answer such a—momentous—question."

He smiled. "I cannot quarrel with you there." He appeared to have regained his composure. "I can only say, Lady Jane, that I have the greatest admiration and respect for you." He placed his hands on her shoulders. "I shall do everything in my power to please you," he said, and bent his head and kissed her gently.

Jane stood quietly, and when he raised his head and looked down into her eyes, they were curiously calm. There was nothing on her face to indicate the vivid, mysterious resistance that he sensed deep within her.

It was that feeling of resistance that so disconcerted him and not Jane's plea for more time. Anne was aware of his distress and set herself to reassure him. Jane, she told him, was of all human creatures the one over whom habit had most power and novelty least. She could tolerate nothing she was not used to and the very fact that she was willing to give him an opportunity to pursue their friendship was very encouraging.

Mr. Wrexham grew more cheerful as he listened to Anne. He thought he began to understand Jane's attitude. He thought of her as one who had never thought much on the subject of love. She was, after all, very young. Doubtless her innocence had prevented her from understanding his attentions. She had been overpowered by the suddenness of a proposal so wholly unexpected.

Julian Wrexham was not a man to underrate his own attraction. It must follow, he thought, that with a little perseverence on his part he should succeed. Jane's initial fastidiousness did her no harm in his eyes. In fact, there was a new attraction in the idea of adding to his collection of choice objects a young lady who was not overly eager to accept the first offer made to her. It would be proper that the woman he might marry should behave in such a restrained fashion.

Jane went directly to her room after she had

left Julian Wrexham. She crossed the polished floor to her favorite windowseat and sat down, drawing her legs up under her. It was raining and she stared out at the drenched garden, her face as bleak as the scene before her.

For almost the first time in her life, Jane was afraid. She had suspected for some time the Marquis's purpose in bringing her to London. Even Jane's armor had not been proof against the gossip and the innuendoes that had surrounded her at every social gathering she attended. It was quite clear that London expected her to marry and to marry well. It was now clear that her uncle expected the same.

Jane rested her forehead on her knees and closed her eyes. In the sudden dark the rain sounded even louder. She thought of her past years, years spent moored to a growing boy with golden eyes and streaked blond hair. Jane's whole life belonged to David. It had never occurred to her that she would ever be parted from him. Painful as they had been, their previous separations had been bearable because they were temporary. Whenever she had felt the emptiness of his absence most acutely, she had pretended that he was only in the next room; that she would be seeing him momentarily. And they had always written to each other.

Her months in London had jolted Jane out of the complacency of childhood and forced her to look beyond the present moment. For the first time she faced the future as an adult, and she was frightened.

Her uncle would never let her marry David. Jane had learned enough about the ways of the world to realize how the world would look upon such an alliance. And she was unsure of David's feelings. Would he want to marry her?

As she sat with her head bowed, listening to the rain, Jane was sure of only one thing. A future without David was impossible. "I should be so lonely," she whispered to herself. "So terribly lonely."

Chapter XVI

This bud of love, by summer's ripening breath,
May prove a beauteous flower. . . .
  —William Shakespeare

In Jane's mind there were two primary goals to aim for. First, she must not alarm her uncle or Anne by raising suspicions about her feelings. With this end in mind, she had been careful to refrain from talking about David. For this reason also she had not rejected Julian Wrexham outright. If she had, her uncle would have wanted to know why. All Jane wanted to do at this point was to buy time. In May, they would be going to Newmarket for the races and Jane would achieve her second goal. She had to see David.

For the first time in her life, Jane dissimulated. She accompanied Anne to Almacks and allowed Julian Wrexham to take her driving in the Park. She was pleasant, agreeable, and surprisingly social. She never mentioned David.

The Marquis was pleased, at first. But as this most unJane-like behavior continued, he began to be suspicious. "What's the matter with her?" he complained to Anne. "She agreed to join Wrexham's party at the opera tomorrow night. The opera! She hates music."

"Really, Edward," Anne said with some amusement, "you are difficult to please. First you complain of Jane's unsociability. Now, when she has apparently mended her ways, you complain about that. Really, my dear, you must strive for more consistency."

The Marquis had just returned from White's and he looked very elegant in his well-cut coat of blue superfine. But there was a frown between his black brows. "The opera, Anne!" he said. "I don't think even David could get Jane to the opera."

There was dead silence as they looked at each other, each realizing the significance of that last remark. Then Lord Rayleigh said heavily, "I don't know what she's thinking, Anne, that's the trouble. Jane was always clear as water; not now." He walked to the fireplace and stared into the grate. "She never mentions him. That isn't natural. Even if she were in love with Wrexham, she would not cease to mention David."

Anne looked at her hands, folded over the embroidery in her lap. "No," she said.

"What am I to do?" He sounded suddenly tired.

Anne, who had come to understand Jane better than she was willing to admit, looked grave. "If she does indeed love David, I don't know what you can do, Edward. Jane is not an ordinary young girl, easily swayed by the opinion of her family. I would not do anything rash at the moment, however. If you sent David away, for example, you might end up precipitating exactly what it is you hope to avoid."

He sighed. "I know."

She smiled encouragingly. "Who knows, if Jane is willing to go to the opera with Mr. Wrexham, she might be more enthralled than we give her credit for."

"Let us hope so, Anne," was his unenthusiastic reply.

It was May when the Rayleighs, with Jane and Julian Wrexham, returned to Heathfield. It was Anne's idea to invite Wrexham. She and Lord Rayleigh hoped that continued association with his undeniable charm would produce the desired result in Jane.

The Marquis normally had a houseful of company during race weeks, but Anne's condition caused him to cancel the usual houseparty. He had also decided, David or no David, to stay at Heathfield for the rest of the summer. The exertion of chaperoning Jane was too much for Anne at present.

The invitation to Julian Wrexham and his acceptance was as good as an engagement announcement. Jane did not care. All she wanted was to get home to David. She would have agreed to the whole Wrexham family if it got her what she wanted.

They arrived late in the afternoon. The Marquis expected Jane to run immediately to the stables, but she surprised him. She very graciously showed Julian Wrexham over the house and spent the evening after dinner talking to him in the drawing room. Lord Rayleigh began to wonder if he had misjudged the situation.

He would not have wondered if he had seen the note she had dispatched by one of the footmen. He delivered it to David's cottage after the dinner hour. It read simply, "Meet me tomorrow at nine o'clock at the lake. Jane."

She was at the stables before eight, missing David, who was out on the heath. She had planned it that way; she wanted to see him alone. Consequently; she reached the lake long before he did and sat staring at the water, her unquiet mind out of tune with the serenity of her surroundings.

David was scarcely less agitated. He had heard about Julian Wrexham; the family had not been in residence above an hour when hints of marriage were flying around the servants' quarters. When David had gotten Jane's note, he feared she wanted to be the one to tell him about her engagement.

As he came out of the woods the sight of her slender back and black head clawed at his heart with sudden savage pain. His hands clenched momentarily. "Why the elaborate secrecy, Jane?" he finally managed to say.

At the sound of that deep, quiet voice the tension inside of Jane seemed to shatter. She jumped to her feet with the free, unhampered agility of a boy. "David!" Her eyes glowed as she moved toward him.

Involuntarily, he took a step toward her, then checked himself. "I should be supervising the exercise gallops," he said doggedly, determined to get the worst over with. "Why did you drag me out here this morning?"

His words were hardly welcoming and the light died out of her eyes. She began to look anxious. "I had to see you alone, David. Something terrible has happened." She swallowed. "They want me to get married. That's why they insisted I go to London with them."

He looked at her warily. "I know."

She stared at him in utter stupefaction. "You knew?"

"It was obvious, it seems, to everyone but you."

Temper flared in the aquamarine of her eyes. "You might have shared your wisdom with me."

"Why?"

"Why?" she repeated incredulously. "Because I have no intention of marrying one of those people, that's why. Because I had to spend a miserable couple of months being nice to people I despised. Because I missed you and missed you, and because I was afraid." She stopped, bit her lip, and suddenly turned her back on him.

Deep inside him, David's heart began to thud. "You aren't going to marry this Wrexham fellow?" he asked carefully.

"Of course not." She made a small gesture of arrogance and impatience. "What has he to do with me?"

There was a brief silence. "Turn around, Jane," he said very quietly.

Slowly she obeyed him, her eyes still dark with anger and confusion and pain. She raised them and found his; they were full of comfort and of love. It was suddenly as though the invisible cord that had always bound them was contracting and pulling them closer. "I love you. I have always loved you. Will you marry me?" he said.

The relief she felt was shattering in its intensity. She flung herself into his arms, her own clasped tightly about his neck. "I love *you*," she said fiercely. "No one else. Only you."

He held her close, his cheek against her hair. The slim curves of her body were pressed against him. "Jane," he said. A muscle jumped in the corner of his mouth. "Jane," he said again, more urgently.

She loosened her strangle hold on his neck and raised her head to look at him. Slowly, as though pulled by a force he could not withstand, he bent his head toward hers. His kiss was gentle, his lips cool and firm against hers. She closed her eyes and leaned against him, her hands slipping around him to rest against his back. She could feel the strong muscles under her palms. David's mouth became harder, more demanding. Her own lips opened willingly and her body arched against him, melting into his limbs and bones. Julian Wrexham's kiss had been an invasion; something to tolerate for the sake of not raising suspicions. David's kiss roused sensations she had not known existed. Her surroundings disappeared. The only thing left in the world was David and what he was making her feel.

Suddenly, two hard hands grasped her shoulders and put her away from him. Surprised, she opened her eyes and stared up at him. He was breathing as though he had been running and his eyes were slits of molten gold. "God, Jane," he said, his voice rougher than she had ever heard it. "Don't tempt me like this. It isn't fair."

His hands bit into the soft flesh of her upper arms, but she made no complaint. For the first time Jane understood what marriage with David would mean. Her eyes were dark and heavy; she looked like one who is suddenly wakened. They stared at each other for a long minute and passion beat in the air between them. Then Jane whispered, "What are we going to do? Uncle Edward will never let me marry you."

Her voice broke the spell that seemed to hold them. He dropped his hands from her arms and stepped back. "I know," he said in a more normal voice. "We shall have to elope."

"I thought of that. But we are both under age. Who would marry us?"

He smiled at her candid "I thought of that." She looked so beautiful that he took another step back before saying, "We'll have to go to Scotland, Jane. Minors can be legally married there."

She looked at him in admiration. "I didn't know that. Scotland. All right. When?"

He laughed at that, for sheer joy. "Aren't you even worried about how we are going to live?"

"No," she answered, perfectly soberly. "I don't care where or how we live. I only care that I'm with you."

David's mouth looked suddenly very tender. "I know," he said gently. "If I didn't believe that I wouldn't do what I'm going to do. You will sacrifice wealth, luxury, and position if you marry me, Jane."

"I don't care," she said.

"I know," he said again. His voice became more businesslike. "Two things may happen. Lord Rayleigh may fire me and throw the both of us out of Heathfield. If he does that, I am pretty sure of being able to find another job as Head Trainer. We can sell the cottage and buy another one, if we have to. On the other hand, he may allow me to stay. I hope he does. He pays me a good salary and I have some money saved. We should be able to make it, Jane."

Her extraordinary light eyes were blazing with excitement. "David, I have money. Or I will have when I'm twenty-one."

He looked startled. "You will? How much?"

"Eighty thousand pounds."

"What!"

"Yes. My father and mother left it to me."

"I didn't know that." He sounded subdued.

"I didn't either until this year. Don't you see? We can buy our own stud, raise our own horses. We just have to wait four more years."

"Eighty thousand pounds," he said.

She looked at him narrowly. "David Chance, if you make a fuss about spending my money, I'll never speak to you again."

He laughed unwillingly. "But don't you see, Jane. People will think I'm a fortune hunter."

"Nobody who matters will think that, and you will just have to put up with it if they do. It doesn't make any sense to work for someone else if you can work for yourself." She looked again at his unhappy face. "Oh, for heaven's sake, David, I'll give it all to charity if it bothers you that much."

He smiled at her wryly. "Would you?"

"Of course I would," she answered instantly.

He laughed shakenly and reached for her once again. He held her tightly for a moment, his mouth buried in the shining smoothness of her hair. Then he said, "If you are willing to be poor for me, I suppose I must be willing to be rich for you." Resolutely he put her away from him. "It will take a few weeks to arrange everything. I want to leave the stable in order."

Jane saw nothing odd in being asked to postpone her elopement for the convenience of a few horses. "Of course," she agreed. "Do you want me to do anything?"

"No. Just try not to act suspiciously. I think Lord Rayleigh is uneasy about us already."

She smiled complacently. "I have been very clever, David," she assured him. "I purposely did not refuse Mr. Wrexham's proposal and I have

been very nice to him since then. I'm sure Uncle
Edward and Anne are confident they will soon be
announcing our engagement. I ought to go on the
stage, I've been so convincing," said Jane with mis-
placed self-congratulations.

David's amber eyes glowed with amusement,
but he did not question her further. They decided to see each other as infrequently as possible
in the company of others. Jane promised to meet
him at his cottage before dinner each day, a time
when she could conveniently disappear for an
hour or so. They would have to be satisfied with
that for a few more weeks at least.

Chapter XVII

O villain, villain, smiling, damned villain!
—William Shakespeare

Jane took Julian Wrexham to the stables on the afternoon of their first day back at Heathfield. They walked down the gravel drive together and the tall, fair-haired man and the slender black-haired girl made a picture that caused every stablehand who saw them to smile paternally. Mr. Wrexham looked like the sort of man who should be Lady Jane's husband.

David was out at one of the paddocks and Jane had taken her suitor around the stables before he returned. They were standing in the yard when he came through the door in the far wing which led out to the heath. Jane called to him and he came unhurriedly across the yard to meet them. He looked faintly ironic at Jane's introduction of him as "My uncle's trainer and one of my oldest friends," but he nodded pleasantly at Mr. Wrexham and asked if there was anything else he might like to see.

David was slightly taller than Wrexham and as he looked up into the gold-flecked amber eyes of Lord Rayleigh's trainer the expression on his face froze. Jane was too preoccupied to notice; her own vivid face and brilliant eyes attested to the secret delight she was hugging to herself. David looked curiously at the man who wanted to marry Jane and saw only the elegant bones and gray eyes of a born aristocrat. He glanced quickly at Jane, saw the look on her face, and hurried into speech. "Do you and Mr. Wrexham want to ride out, Jane?"

"Yes. I thought I would take Mr. Wrexham over to Marren Hill." She looked alarmingly like a small girl bent on mischief, and David turned away before he had to smile back at her.

"A good idea," he said. "I'll see to the horses. Mr. Wrexham," he nodded again to Jane's companion, who had not said a word, and disappeared into the stable.

Julian Wrexham was unusually silent as they rode across the heath, but as Jane was unusually chatty, she didn't notice. She was glad to be home, glad to be out on the heath, glad most of all because of David. Some of her happiness spilled over to include Mr. Wrexham, and she talked enthusiastically the whole way.

They reached the bottom of Marren Hill and Jane said, "David and I used to picnic here all the time when we were children. There is an old quarry on the other side. The view from the top is really lovely."

"You have known David all your life, I gather," he said in a rather restrained tone.

"Yes. Ever since I came to live with my uncle when I was six. We grew up together."

There was a pause, then Julian Wrexham said, "Would you like to climb the hill with me? I would enjoy seeing the view."

Jane looked doubtfully at his immaculate buckskin breeches. "It is rather a rough climb," she said.

He smiled. "I don't mind if you don't."

They dismounted, tied up the horses, and Jane had to admit he managed the steep path quite creditably. He admired the view profusely and looked with interest at the steep, sheer drop of the quarry to the rocky hillside below. They sat down beneath one of the beech trees and he said to her casually, "Just who is David—Chance, did you say?"

Jane looked surprised and then wary. "David is my uncle's trainer, Mr. Wrexham."

He looked at her face and a charming smile suddenly lit his own. "I don't mean to pry," he said. "I am just surprised to find such a young boy in a position of such responsibility. Is he really in charge of all your uncle's horses?"

He had taken exactly the right tack. Jane discoursed for many minutes on the quality of her uncle's horses and David's undisputed brilliance in handling them. "He has been in sole charge for six months now, ever since Tuft retired. Uncle Edward is very pleased with him," she concluded.

"Was David's father a groom also?" he asked.

"No, David's father was the steward of a great estate in France. He was killed in the revolution. David's aunt brought him to England seventeen years ago and they have lived in Newmarket ever since."

"I see. He lives with his aunt, then."

"His aunt died a few years ago. He lives alone now, in that cottage closest to Heathfield on the Newmarket Road."

"His mother is dead also?"

Jane was surprised by his curiosity, but she answered readily enough. "Yes. She died in France soon after David was born."

He smiled once again at her puzzled face. "I number several French émigrés among my closest friends, so I am always interested in the subject. What part of France was David's family from?"

"Artois."

He bowed his head for a minute and when he looked up his gray eyes were darker than usual. "That cursed revolution has caused much suffering for many people," he said soberly.

Jane, who could only approve of a revolution that had brought her David, did not reply, and in a few minutes they were preparing to retrace their steps down the hill and back toward Heathfield.

Race week at Newmarket was as colorful, exciting, and busy as ever. The Marquis's horses did very well, particularly the three-year-olds. There was only one incident to mar the smooth surface of the week; someone tried to tamper with Pericles, Lord Rayleigh's most promising three-year-old. David discovered it when he went to check on the horses, as he invariably did the night before a race.

David slept above the stable during race week. A great deal of money changed hands at Newmarket and he was conscious of the not infrequent attempts that had been made in the past to bribe the stableboys to give a horse a bucketful of water before a race or to slip a drug into its feed. A favorite who did not win could make someone a tidy sum of money. David felt happier being close enough to keep an eye on the stable, night and day.

Everyone else was in bed and asleep when David made his final rounds at about eleven o'clock. It was part of his routine so the man whom he surprised outside of Pericles's stall was obviously unfamiliar with his schedule.

Pericles's stall was the last one on the lefthand row, directly before the tack room. David unlatched the lower part of the stall door and bent to put his lantern down when something hit him hard on the back of the head. He pitched to the ground and lay still. The dark figure of the attacker raised its arm again, but Pericles lashed out with his teeth over the open top half of the stall and the intruder backed off. The upset thoroughbred then crashed his hoofs into the door, knocking it into David's unconscious body. The horse whistled shrilly and as there was a sound of running feet the intruder melted back into the darkness of the tack room.

The whole family was at breakfast the next

morning when McAllister, the butler, informed them of the previous night's disturbance. All the color drained from Jane's face. "Is he all right?" she demanded fiercely.

"Yes, Lady Jane," McAllister answered reassuringly. "Stubbs took him home and fetched the doctor. He told Mr. David to keep to his bed this morning, but otherwise he is fine."

Without a word Jane put down her napkin, rose from the table, and left the room. There was a grim line around Lord Rayleigh's mouth as he said to Julian Wrexham, "I must apologize for my niece. David is like a brother to her and she is naturally concerned about him."

"I perfectly understand," Wrexham replied graciously. "There is no need to apologize."

But the grim line did not relax around the Marquis's mouth. Mr. Wrexham did not perfectly understand Jane's behavior; Lord Rayleigh was afraid that *he* did.

Jane took the shortcut through the Home Woods that brought her to David's cottage in ten minutes. She opened the front door, out of breath and flushed from running, and found Mrs. Copley tidying up the big front room. "Lady Jane!" she said, clearly startled by Jane's sudden appearance.

"How is he, Mrs. Copley?" she asked urgently.

"Jane." It was David's voice calling her from the bedroom and without waiting for an answer to her question Jane went unhesitatingly toward the door on the right that led, she knew, to David's bedroom.

He was dressed in a white shirt and buckskins, lying quietly on top of his made-up bed. There was a plaster patch on the back of his head and he was pale, but otherwise he looked normal. She stood at the foot of the bed, staring at him like a tiger whose only cub has been threatened. "Are you all right?"

He smiled at her expression. "Yes."

She took a few steps forward so that she stood beside him. "What happened, David?" she asked tensely.

In a perfectly calm, expressionless tone, he told her. When he finished, Jane frowned at him. "But David, if the intruder wanted to harm the horses, why didn't he just wait until after you had finished your rounds? Why did he attack you?"

"He must have feared I would discover him."

"He was safe if he was hiding in the tack room. You had no reason to go in there."

"No, but our friend couldn't know that."

Jane continued to stare at him, worry making her eyes look more green than blue. David held a hand out to her. "Don't upset yourself so, love," he said in a deep, quiet voice. "It was an unpleasant thing to happen, but the horses are all right and all I've got is a bump on my head. There's no cause for you to worry."

She held his hand tightly between her own for a brief moment, her eyes on his face. A spark of something that was not worry awoke in their blue-green depths and she was raising his hand to her lips when Mrs. Copley came to the door of the room. Jane stayed on for a few more minutes before David sent her away.

Chapter XVIII

O villainy! Ho! let the door be lock'd:
Treachery! Seek it out.
 —William Shakespeare

On the last day of the Newmarket Meet, Laura Rivingdale sought out David. She had not seen him since the previous spring and had resolved to put him out of her mind. She had met Julian Wrexham, however, and was anxious to see how the looming probability of Jane's engagement to him had affected David.

David was standing watching one of the grooms walk Minette, a lovely Arab mare who had just taken a second place, when Laura found him. His eyes were slightly narrowed against the sun, his hands thrust casually into the pockets of his buckskin breeches. The day was warm and he had removed his jacket. His immaculate white shirt fit comfortably across the breadth of his shoulders and contrasted sharply with the golden brown column of his neck.

"David," she said softly.

He turned at the sound of his name and at the sight of her, surprise flickered in his eyes. "Mrs. Rivingdale," he said steadily.

Her own eyes narrowed, but she continued pleasantly, "How have you been?"

"Very well, thank you." He glanced at the discreetly interested grooms and walked over to stand beside her. "Are you enjoying the races?" he asked courteously. "Let me show you around the stable area." Without waiting for her reply, he began to walk away from the Rayleigh area; she followed without protest. When they were out of the sight of his men, David halted. "What is the matter with you, Laura?" he demanded angrily. "What would your husband say if he knew you were wandering around alone like this?"

She shrugged. "I don't care and to be perfectly honest, neither does George. I wanted to see you."

"Why?" he asked abruptly.

She stared at him for a minute, wishing he were not so beautiful, that her desire for him was not such a burden upon her. "I understand Jane is soon to be married," she said finally.

A look of faint amusement came across David's bronzed, faintly remote face. "Yes," he said. "So I believe."

She bit her lip. "I told you how it would be."

"Yes," he agreed politely, "you told me." The anguish her words had brought him seemed very far off now and he could regard her with more compassion than he had previously. "You should not have sought me out, Laura. Your husband may be somewhat complaisant, but he would not tolerate his wife having an *affaire* with a stableboy. No one knows about us. Let us keep it that way."

He looked at her seriously. "You know what I say is true."

She did, but it didn't seem important. Jealousy stabbed her. "You don't believe Jane will marry him," she accused.

There was a brief silence, then David spoke and his deep, quiet voice held a distinct note of danger. "This is not a subject I will discuss with you, Laura. Now or ever. Do I make myself clear?"

Her eyes dropped before the look in his. "Yes," she said breathlessly. "Quite clear."

"Good. I will leave you to find your own way back. I must prepare Pericles for the next race." He looked at her steadily. "Goodbye, Laura."

She turned and walked away, her head high and her back straight. But her cheeks were burning and suspicion smoldered in her heart.

She and her husband were guests at Heathfield for dinner that evening and Laura was keenly aware of Jane. Jane wore one of her new gowns, an almond-green cambric muslin that was surprisingly elegant. Her behavior during dinner was impeccable. She discussed the day's racing with Julian Wrexham and George Rivingdale, who sat on either side of her, and both men attended to what she said with unfeigned interest. She appeared to be on perfectly comfortable terms with Wrexham, but there was no special warmth in the clear, clipped tones of her voice when she addressed him.

When the ladies withdrew to leave the gentlemen to their wine, Laura tried to draw Jane out upon the subject of Wrexham. Mrs. Rivingdale prided herself upon her social finesse and inquired in an entirely unexceptional manner. Anne flushed, conscious that Laura only assumed what all the world must, that there would shortly be an engagement announcement appearing in the *Times*. She hesitated, trying to find a tactful way of replying. Jane, to whom tact was a foreign language, merely looked with raised eyebrows at Laura Rivingdale. "When I get engaged or married, I shall be sure to inform all the proper authorities, Mrs. Rivingdale," she said flatly. "At present I am neither and I do not at all care to speculate on the future."

"Jane!" Anne said in some distress.

Jane shrugged. "I'm sure Mrs. Rivingdale isn't in the least interested in my activities, Anne. She was merely trying to be polite. Are you returning to London or do you make a stay at Hailsham Lodge?" she asked Laura determinedly.

Laura handled very well the rapier thrust of conversation in a curious and malicious society; Jane's weapon, however, was not the rapier but the battle ax. "We return to London, Lady Jane," she replied faintly, tacitly relinquishing the field. When she left Heathfield a few hours later, she was still in ignorance as to the true state of Jane's feelings.

David and Jane planned to elope two weeks after Newmarket's Race Week. David was quietly withdrawing what money he had from the bank and inquiring into the possibilities of selling the cottage. He also spent a good deal of time in mapping out the route they would take to Scotland. He wanted to avoid the main roads in order to cut down on their chances of being overtaken.

A week before they were due to leave, Jane was cutting through the Home Woods on her way to the cottage. It was six o'clock and she wanted a few minutes alone with David before she had to return to Heathfield and dress for dinner. Jane usually slipped out the side door at about this time every evening; the servants were at dinner and no one saw her go or return.

She was moving swiftly along a narrow path through the trees when she came around a turn and saw David on the path some forty yards before her. He was walking quickly, bent on the same destination as she, and as she watched he slowed down suddenly. She was about to call to him when two things happened simultaneously. He bent his head to look at something on the ground and a shot rang out. David dropped to the path. Jane screamed and ran toward him. Dimly she was aware of the sound of someone moving through the trees on her right. "Don't shoot!" she shouted. "There are people here!"

David rose as she reached him and as she began to say his name he grabbed her and threw her to the ground, covering her body with his own.

Jane's heart was hammering so hard she could feel it in her head. She lay on her stomach, her cheek against the dirt path. She didn't move. At last David lifted himself off of her and cautiously looked around. "It's all right now, Jane," he said in a voice he strove to make normal. "You can get up. I'm sorry if I hurt you."

Jane allowed him to help her to her feet and brush some of the dirt off her jacket. He apologized again, and again asked if he had hurt her. When she didn't respond, he had to finally look up and meet her eyes. They were enormous, dilated with fear. "If you hadn't bent to look at something on the path he would have hit you," she said in a very tight voice.

"It was a stupid poacher." He shrugged. "There's no harm done, luckily."

Jane's eyes never moved from his face. "There are never any poachers in these woods. They are too close to the house." He started to say something, but she shook her head. "It wasn't a poacher, was it, David?" There was a white line around her mouth. Her cheek was scratched from where it had been pressed upon the ground. He reached out and touched it gently.

"No," he said finally. "It wasn't a poacher."

"Then who?"

"I don't know." He looked at her somberly. "Until now, I wasn't really sure, but I'm very much afraid someone is trying to kill me."

What little color there was in her face drained away, making the scratch on her cheek more prominent. "The night you were attacked outside Pericles's stall?" she asked breathlessly.

"That. And when I was out on the heath the

other day, someone loosened my girth strap. As soon as I got into full gallop, it would have given."

She clasped her hands together tensely. "How did you discover it?"

He smiled wryly. "Good habits pay off. I always run my hand under the girth before I mount. It's an automatic gesture; I never even think about it. I had saddled the horse only fifteen minutes before. I went to mount, ran my hand under the saddle, and the girth was loose."

"What else?" she asked tersely.

"When I was in Newmarket the other day, a piece of stone fell from the top of a building and just missed landing on my head."

"Jesus Christ," Jane said, her eyes huge, frightened pools in her ashen face. "And now this. But why, David? And who?"

His mouth set. "I've asked myself that question every day for the last week. I don't know! What possible reason could anyone have to want me dead?"

Jane swallowed. "Oh David, oh David," she whispered, and he stepped forward to take her in his arms.

"I didn't want you to know," he said. "I didn't want to frighten you." He felt her shiver and held her even closer.

"What can we do?" she asked against his shoulder.

"I don't know, love," he replied soberly.

She was still for a minute, acutely conscious of

the warm strength of his body, the steady reassuring beat of his heart.

"I'll tell Uncle Edward," she said with determination.

"No, Jane." He held her away from him. "There is no evidence. He would never believe it." He grimaced. "I can hardly believe it myself. If it wasn't for this feeling I have. . . ."

"What feeling," she prompted when his words trailed off.

"A feeling of danger," he said slowly. "I can sense it. I'm not imagining things; it's there, all right." He looked down at her strained face. "We can't go to your uncle on my feelings, Jane."

"We have to do *something!*" she cried.

"I will be very vigilant, I promise you. Whoever he is must be getting frustrated. He will come out into the open before long, of that I'm sure. When he does, I'll deal with him."

"Let's elope now," she urged. "If you're away from here, he won't know where to find you."

"We would have to return," he said patiently. "And then perhaps you too would be exposed to this—madman. There will be no marriage until I can find out who is responsible for these attacks."

She argued with him for ten minutes, but nothing she could say would change his mind.

Chapter XIX

A little more than kin, and less than kind.
—William Shakespeare

For the three days following the incident in the wood, Jane attached herself to David with grim determination. Her resolution of concealing her love vanished in the face of this threat to his life. Wherever David went, there went Jane. She met him at the stables at six in the morning and rode out with him on all the training gallops. She accompanied him home for lunch and left him, with great reluctance, only to return to Heathfield House for her own dinner at eight.

David expostulated with her in vain. She stared at him with the eyes of a wild thing whose young are in danger, and refused to budge. For the first time he had a taste of the will that Lord Rayleigh knew all too well.

The Marquis tried to reason with her as well. "What is the matter with you, Jane?" he asked her irritably. It was the second day of Jane's self-imposed surveillance, and he had taken her into his study after dinner to try to talk some sense into her.

She had refused to meet his eyes. "There is

156

nothing wrong with me, Uncle Edward," she said tonelessly.

"You have completely neglected Mr. Wrexham these last two days. I understand you have been following David around like a puppy. Well, I won't have it, Jane. Do you hear me?" He was genuinely angry.

Jane looked at him as if she did not know him. "There is nothing you can do about it," she said in the same toneless voice as before.

"I can lock you in your room," the Marquis snapped at her. Jane's eyes narrowed and the Marquis suddenly felt himself outside the bounds of civilization. She looked quite startlingly dangerous.

"If you do that," she said in a voice that was ominously quiet, "you will regret it."

For a perceptible space of time, Lord Rayleigh stared at the fierce, beautiful face of his niece. "Something has happened," he said. "What is it, Jane?"

"I can't tell you, Uncle Edward," she replied, but for the first time there was a tremor in her voice. He moved across to where she stood and put a comforting arm around her. "You can tell me, brat, you know that," he said, and his voice now was gentle. But the slender body within his arm was rigid, refusing to yield to gentleness as well as to threats.

As Lord Rayleigh did not, in fact, have the nerve to lock her in her room, her surveillance of David continued. The Marquis was only thankful that Mr. Wrexham, who had certainly noticed the drastic change in Jane's behavior, never mentioned it. On the contrary, to the great relief of the Marquis and Anne, he had the tact to announce that he was going on a few days' visit to a friend of his who lived in the neighboring county of Cambridgeshire. When he left the following afternoon after lunch, Lord and Lady Rayleigh breathed a collective sigh of relief. Now at least they would be able to deal with Jane without the disturbing presence of her would-be fiancé in the house.

David left the stable later than usual that evening. The sky had been overcast all day and the smell of rain was in the air. Jane had been prevailed on to leave him at four o'clock that afternoon. She was exhausted and David had promised not to leave the company of one of the grooms until it was time for him to go home.

He had been returning to the cottage by different routes each day and today took him back through the woods for the first time since the shooting incident. He approached the cottage from the side and entered by a window rather than the front door. The room was empty. David checked the two bedrooms before he came back to the oven where a pot was simmering. For the first time he noticed a paper on the table. He picked it up and read with astonishment: "David. I know who it is. Meet me on top of Marren Hill immediately. Jane."

Deep surprise ran through David. He took the note closer to the fire and read it again. It was Jane's handwriting, all right, somewhat scrawled as if she had been in a hurry. "I know who it is." That could mean only one thing. David moved swiftly to the door. He would have to cut back to the stables to get a horse.

By the time he reached Marren Hill the gray clouds had turned to black. There was no sign of Jane's mare tied anywhere at the foot of the hill, and for the first time David felt an apprehension of danger. But the handwriting was hers. With a fear that turned his mouth dry, he wondered if Jane herself was in peril.

There was only one way to find out. Swiftly, David began to climb the hill.

When he was a little way from the top, he halted. He could see nothing in the increasing darkness. Carefully he pushed on, until he was standing on the flat crest of the hill, sheltered from the gusting wind by the beech trees that grew along its rim. There was no one there. He called, "Jane!" He turned to look out across the heath, straining to see her figure somewhere.

"She isn't coming," said the mellow, pleasant voice of Julian Wrexham. David whirled around and found himself staring into the barrel of a very competent-looking pistol. He raised his head slowly and met the gray eyes of Julian Wrexham. His own eyes widened. He looked from Wrexham to the thicket where he had evidently been hidden, then back to Wrexham again.

"You are surprised to see me?" Wrexham asked scornfully. "I was afraid you had realized I must be the one behind all your recent 'accidents.' After all, they started only after I arrived at Heathfield."

David's eyes were gold in the wary stillness of his face. "I had thought of that," he said evenly, "but I could not imagine what your motive might be."

Wrexham's thin nostrils flared slightly. "I could not allow you to take what was mine."

Sudden comprehension flickered in David's eyes. "Jane," he said slowly.

Wrexham looked surprised, then a malicious smile crossed his face. "Jane, of course," he agreed smoothly. He raised the pistol slightly. "It is most unfortunate that I must put a period to this discussion—uh, Chance. You will be found in the quarry—quite dead, I am afraid. Everyone will think you were robbed and killed. I, of course, am visiting my dear friend in Cambridgeshire. I will be so sorry to hear of your demise when I return."

David was frowning, his mind seemingly elsewhere. "The note," he said abruptly. "That was Jane's handwriting."

"Ah, the note." Wrexham looked amused. "Really, it seems I could earn my living as a master forger, should that unlikely need ever arise."

"*You* wrote it?"

"I had a sample of Lady Jane's writing to go by. It is, as you well know, very distinctive. It was not hard to copy."

"She will never marry you, Wrexham." David's voice was surprisingly steady.

"That is a chance I will just have to take," Wrexham replied, a strange glint in his eyes.

David had been staring at Wrexham with unwavering attention; now his eyes suddenly swung beyond the other man's shoulder and widened with surprised recognition. For a fraction of a minute Wrexham's head turned and in that space of time David dove at him.

The gun went off, but David had thrown him off balance and the shot went wide. In a minute the two men were locked in a deadly struggle.

Julian Wrexham prided himself on his excellent physique, which he kept by regular exercise. One of his recreations was to work out at Gentleman Jackson's Boxing Saloon whenever he was in London. He was very good.

David had learned to fight in the stables of Newmarket, where there were no rules but winning. His body had been hardened and strengthened by years of hard work. They were very much of a height, and very evenly matched.

For what seemed like forever they grappled together, then Wrexham, using a movement he had learned from Jackson himself, bent sharply and somersaulted David to the ground. David did not try to rise, and as Wrexham came at him he used the side of his hand, hard as cast iron, to chop at the other man's exposed throat. Wrexham staggered back, gagging, and David surged to his feet like a cat and flung himself at his attacker.

Wrexham saw him coming and backed away from him, his hands still at his injured throat. "Wrexham!" David called suddenly as he saw the danger the other man did not. Their struggle had taken them very close to the edge of the quarry. David stopped his own headlong rush as he saw where it was leading him, but Julian Wrexham was backing up. He never knew he was close to the edge of the quarry until he stepped over it. Then he screamed.

Breathing hard, with white face and dilated eyes, David looked down the sheer rock face of the cliff. There was an outcrop of rock three quarters of the way down. The breath shuddered in David's throat as he saw that Wrexham was lying there. He was not moving.

The evening was cool, but there was sweat on David's forehead. He sat down suddenly and dropped his head between his hands. When the attack of nausea was over, he rose and began to descend the hill. He would have to go home for a rope. Whatever Wrexham had tried to do, he couldn't leave a hurt man lying alone like that all night. If he wasn't dead now, he would be by morning.

It was raining by the time David got back to the cottage. He fetched a rope from the shed and a lantern as well. Night was coming fast and with the rain there would be no moon.

The rain was falling steadily when he returned to Marren Hill. Looping the rope over his shoulder, David took the lantern and started to climb.

When he reached the top he held the lantern over the quarry; dimly he could make out the shadow of the outcrop. He sat down to knot footholds at intervals in the length of rope. Then he tied it around the trunk of one of the beeches and dropped it over the side of the quarry. He set the lantern down and slid over the edge and into the darkness of the quarry.

He reached the rock outcrop without difficulty and, with eyes now accustomed to the darkness, bent to look at Julian Wrexham. He was lying at a peculiar angle; it did not take David long to realize that his neck had been broken.

David pulled himself back up the rope, much faster than he would have if he had had a body to carry. For the second time that night he climbed down Marren Hill, returning this time to the Heathfield stables where he unsaddled and stabled his horse. Mercifully, he saw no one. Then, his face bleak and hard, he set off toward home.

Chapter XX

But passion lends them power, time means. . . .
—William Shakespeare

Jane had been exhausted all day. The strain and
tension she had been under since David was shot
at in the woods finally caught up with her. After
dinner she pleaded a headache and went to bed.
Miss Kilkelly was waiting for her, and Jane allowed her old nurse to undress her and tuck her
into bed. But after Miss Kilkelly had left, Jane
found she could not sleep. Some kind of alarm
within her was sounding, telling her that all was
not well with David. After a few minutes she got
up, took off the nightgown she had just donned,
and pulled an old dress, left from her pre-London
wardrobe, over her head. She threw a cloak
around her head and shoulders and stealthily left
her room, closing the door quietly behind her.

She slipped down the back stairs and saw one of
the footman in the hall. "John," she whispered urgently.

He started when he saw her, but came quickly
to her side. "Yes, Lady Jane?"

"I have to go out," she said softly. "Secretly.

Will you leave the side door open tonight so I can get back in?"

The footman, a middle-aged man who had known Jane since she was six, never hesitated. "Of course, Lady Jane. But will you be all right?"

She smiled reassuringly. "I'll be fine. Don't worry, and don't tell anyone I've gone." She walked to the side door and exited into the rain without a backward glance.

Twenty minutes later she was at the cottage. The front door was locked, so she entered through the same window as David had. The room was empty and his dinner, untouched, lay congealing on the stove.

Her face like stone, Jane set about feeding the fire in the main room and building one in David's bedroom. She had known something was wrong. She would wait one hour, and if David had still not returned she would tell her uncle and start a search.

It was twenty minutes before she heard his steps at the front door. The key turned in the lock and he came in, blinking in the sudden light of the room. "Jane!" His voice sounded strange—harsh and strained. He was soaking wet.

"What happened?" she asked, her own voice far from normal.

"I had an encounter with my saboteur," he spoke with difficulty. "It was Wrexham." Then, controlling visibly all his sense of horror, "He is dead. I killed him."

Jane seemed not to notice what he was saying.

"You're freezing." She pulled a chair up before the fire. "Come and sit down here." He came across the room slowly, like a man in a daze. Obediently he sat in the chair she had set for him. She stood before him. "Wrexham," she said on a long note of surprise. "And he is dead?"

He looked up at her, seeing her clearly for the first time since he had come in. Her unbound hair hung heavy and straight almost to her waist. She glowed in the firelight, black and ivory, warm and living. He had been so close to the edge of death; he had almost lost her forever.

Jane returned his look and for a minute they were suspended in time as the seconds ticked by unregarded. Then David reached for her and she felt his arms go about her in a desperate grip. She pressed her cheek against his rain-dark head, her own arms straining him against her. David's mouth was buried in the softness of her throat; she could feel fire coursing through her from his wild kisses. Then his grip on her shifted and he was on his feet, swinging her up into his arms.

He carried her into his own bedroom and laid her down on the old-fashioned bed. His breathing was hurried, his eyes narrow, pure gold and filled with desire. Jane looked up at him and slowly began to unbutton her dress. In her haste she had not put on anything under it.

The sight of her white beauty, gleaming in the soft firelight, broke David's last restraint. His hands went to his belt.

There was no love in David's face nor in the

mouth, hard and hungry, that came down on hers. The pentup passion of months had been released by the violence of the night; in David's mouth and hands there was only the urgency of a terrible need.

Jane understood. His hunger did not frighten her. This was David, and whatever he wanted of her she was prepared to give. She made no sound and the slender body he was handling so roughly did not flinch, even when he hurt her. When he finally lay still, his head on her breast, she murmured softly, "Go to sleep, David. Go to sleep, my love. Everything is all right now." Her hand lightly stroked his still-damp hair. But long after he had fallen into the deep sleep of utter exhaustion, Jane lay awake revolving in her mind what David had told her of Julian Wrexham.

When David awoke the rain had passed and moonlight was shining in the window of his bedroom. He lay still for a minute, bewildered, then memory returned. Cautiously he raised himself and looked at Jane. She was sleeping peacefully, all silver and shadow in the moonlight. As he watched her, David's mouth was severe with pain. The memory of his frantic possession of her pierced his mind and caused him to shut his eyes. He shook his head as if in denial. No. It could never have happened.

When he opened his eyes again, Jane was stirring, as if disturbed by his distress. He watched her, his heart hammering. If she should turn from him in revulsion. . . .

Her eyes opened and she looked at him. There was surprise, then, as her own memory came back, her face altered. She looked wary and slightly guilty, like a small girl caught out in mischief who is afraid of being punished. "Are you angry with me?" she asked, lying still against the pillow.

He stared at her in utter stupefaction. When he could speak, he said in a low, difficult voice, "It is I who should be asking you that question."

The moonlight kindled a blue-green spark within her great light eyes. "I won't be angry with you if you won't be angry with me," she offered.

"I hurt you." His voice was curiously rough, as if he were trying to control some powerful emotion. There was a white line around his mouth.

"That doesn't matter," she said impatiently.

"I think it does." He looked grim.

"David, I could have stopped you if I had wanted to." There was a pause, then she said flatly, "I didn't want to, you know."

He looked at her for a minute in silence and the glimmer of a smile lightened his grim young mouth. "We will have to get married now."

"That is a point of view I can only agree with," Jane said approvingly. She propped herself up on the pillows, a quilt pulled up to her chin against the cool night air. "What happened last night?" she asked practically.

He told her, leaning on an elbow and watching her face. He omitted only one thing. Jane went for it like a homing pigeon. "But why, David? Why did Mr. Wrexham want to kill you?"

"I don't know, Jane," he answered calmly. "He neglected to tell me."

"But it doesn't make any sense!" She was frowning with concentration. "It certainly couldn't have been a whim."

"I shouldn't think so, but I'm afraid we'll never know now."

Jane was still frowning. "David, do you think he could have suspected about you and me?"

The last thing David wanted was Jane's blaming herself for what had happened. "I don't see how he possibly could, Jane."

"I don't either," she said thoughtfully. "I was very careful. Besides," she turned to look into his face, "he didn't feel that strongly about me. I would kill for you and you for me, but not Wrexham. He liked me well enough. He thought I was pretty. But he didn't love me like that."

It was David's turn to frown. What she said made sense. But if not for Jane, then why? "All I can think of, Jane, was that the man was mad."

"Well, mad or not, I'm glad he's dead. I was thinking about it last night, and I think we should just wait until someone finds his body. Did anyone see you last night?"

"I don't think so. No."

"Good. Then there's absolutely no reason for anyone to connect you with Wrexham's death. We shall just play dumb and let the storm blow over us."

"I hate to think of him lying there," David said hesitatingly.

"I don't," Jane answered flatly. "In fact, I think I know perfectly how Creon felt when he decreed that Polynices' body should be left unburied for the dogs and birds to eat."

"Jane!" He was half laughing, half appalled. "You don't mean that."

"I do," she said somberly. Her eyes rested possessively on him. "He tried to kill you," she said. "I would like to tear his heart out."

She meant it. As he looked at her beautiful, in-placable face in the moonlight, he remembered clearly his own emotions of the previous evening. "When I saw Wrexham's body lying there on the outcrop, I was terrified," he told her. "All I could think of was it might have been me. And if it were, I should never see you again."

Her voice was constricted. "I know. How do you think I have felt these last few days? At least you would be dead. *I* should have to go on living without you."

"Don't." Instinctively his hand went out to touch her cheek. They stared at each other, both young faces stamped with an identical look. Then Jane said, her voice low, "Love me, David."

You shouldn't, one part of his brain warned. But, the damage is already done, another, more welcome voice said insistently. Slowly he moved toward her until he was bent over her, his lips very lightly upon hers. As her arms came up to circle his neck, his kiss deepened and his hands began to move caressingly over her body. This time he did love her, with an astonishing heart-stopping tenderness and passion that lifted them both to a crescendo of ecstasy they had never imagined existed.

When at last they lay quietly, still locked together, Jane raised heavy, dazed eyes to look up into his face. She wet her lips and whispered, "I had no idea anything could be like that."

He laughed shakenly. "Neither did I." He kissed her eyelids. "Jane," he said, his voice full of wonder.

Her smile, *his* smile, was as good as a caress. "I love you."

"And I love you."

As they spoke quietly together the light outside the window altered. "David!" Jane said suddenly, noticing it. "The sun is coming up. I have to get home before they miss me."

They agreed, with great reluctance, to postpone their elopement until after the furor about Julian Wrexham had died down. It would not be wise, Jane pointed out determinedly, to do anything that might attract attention to themselves.

She promised to slip out late one evening soon and come to the cottage. He knew he should tell her not to, but he didn't.

Chapter XXI

... more light and light it grows.
—William Shakespeare

Jane slept late the next morning. When she finally arrived in the morning parlor at about ten-thirty, she looked rested and radiant. "You look as if you had a good sleep, Jane," Anne said to her. "Is your headache gone?"

"My headache?" For a moment Jane looked bewildered. Then she smiled. "Oh, yes. My headache. Yes, it is quite gone now."

"Good. Do you have plans for today?" Anne spoke diffidently. Jane had been totally unapproachable for the past few days.

"I thought I'd paint," Jane answered easily, "unless you need me for something, Anne."

"No, I thank you," Anne replied faintly, disconcerted by the radical change in Jane's behavior. "Paint by all means, if that is what you wish to do."

And paint Jane did. To the utter astonishment of the Marquis and of Anne, she never went near the stables or David.

They found Julian Wrexham's body on the afternoon of the following day. His horses, which had been tied up in a wood, broke loose and the driverless phaeton was soon discovered. It took the search party five more hours to discover the body.

They brought it back to Heathfield. David was calm when he heard the news from Lord Rayleigh. After making some arrangements for Wrexham's horses, the Marquis said worriedly, "I only hope this doesn't unduly distress my wife."

"Well, it is not very pleasant, my lord," David replied, "but I should think Jane would be the one to be most upset."

"Jane is not expecting a baby," the Marquis said irritably. "Really, I can't imagine how Wrexham came to have such an accident."

Lord Rayleigh, whose mind was on his own troubles, did not notice how David suddenly went white. "Jane is not expecting a baby," the Marquis had said. In a sudden panic David realized that she very well might be.

It was a contingency he had never thought of. He was, after all, only eighteen years of age. He could have told you anything you needed to know about the breeding of horses; with humans he was not so sure. He only knew he had to talk to Jane immediately.

He got her aside late that afternoon. She had come down to the stables by herself and he dragged her into the tack room, scene of so many of their childhood hours together. "Is anything the matter?" she asked, alarmed by the worried look on his face.

He came straight to the point. "Jane, do you think you could be expecting a baby?"

She looked stunned. "What makes you ask me that?"

"Because it happens," he said, a trifle wildly. "Look at Lady Rayleigh."

Jane's wide eyes remained fixed on his face for a long minute, then she said slowly, "I never thought of that."

"Neither did I," he answered tightly. "But if you are, we can't delay. We must be married immediately."

"For heaven's sake, David, don't panic. It takes a long time to have a baby. Anne has been pregnant for ages and she's not expecting until September. We have plenty of time." He had been holding her slender shoulders between his hands and now his unintentionally hard grip relaxed. She didn't look at all upset, only thoughtful. She continued, "I think I know how one tells if one is going to have a baby, but I'm not quite sure. I shall have to ask Anne."

She looked so slender and delicate and young as she stood before him that David's conscience smote him. "It's all my fault," he said gruffly. "You're too young to have a baby. You don't even like them."

"Don't be so silly." Her enchanting smile lit her eyes. "Uncle Edward and Mr. Wrexham certainly thought I was old enough. Besides," she added positively, "I shall like *your* baby."

He reached out and gathered her into his arms.

With his lips buried in her sweet-smelling hair, he said "I love you."

She closed her eyes and listened to the sound of his heart, so strong and regular under her cheek. "Don't worry, David," she murmured. "My having a baby might actually be rather a good thing. Then nobody could separate us."

He held her closer. "Nobody is going to separate us," he said harshly.

"No one could," she answered contentedly.

Lord Rayleigh sent a courier to Wymondham, the Wrexham family seat in Derby. Two days later he received a note saying that Lord Wymondham was on his way to Newmarket to escort the body of his nephew home for burial.

The next day Lord Wymondham arrived at Heathfield. The inquest had been held the previous day and the verdict had been death by misadventure. Julian Wrexham's body was free to be laid to rest in the land of his ancestors.

Lord Wymondham had arrived home from Russia only the previous week. He was a diplomat of international reputation, an ambassador relied on by whatever government happened to be in power. He was a man whose force of character made an instant impression; no one who met him ever forgot him.

The Marquis escorted him to the small saloon where Julian Wrexham's body lay. The Earl looked at it without changing expression. Later, in the Marquis's study, he accepted a glass of sherry and asked calmly, "What happened?"

Lord Rayleigh told him what little he himself knew. "Why he came to be atop of Marren Hill, my lord, is a mystery. We can only surmise that he was lured there by someone and then ruthlessly pushed into the quarry. I can only say we are all deeply distressed and offer you my most heartfelt sympathy."

The Earl was gazing at his wine. "It is certainly strange, as you say, Lord Rayleigh. Do you have many such incidents in this part of the world?"

"No more than anywhere else in England, my lord," the Marquis answered, his gaze on the other's downlooking face. There was something about the Earl that struck a chord of memory in the Marquis's brain, a nagging familiarity in the tall, broad-shouldered form of the older man. The Earl was extremely good-looking, in his early forties, with brown hair and a strong face with authority clearly stamped on it. It must be the family resemblance between him and Wrexham that made him look so familiar, the Marquis decided.

After another sherry the two men rose. "My wife is lying down, Lord Wymondham," the Marquis apologized. "She will be happy to see you at dinner, however."

"I shall look forward to meeting her," the Earl responded courteously. "And your niece as well."

They were standing in the great hall now, waiting for the housekeeper to come and take Lord

Wymondham to his room. At that moment Jane came in. She had gone into Newmarket to do some shopping for Anne and looked for once elegant and fashionable in her walking dress of French blue cambric. She came forward at her uncle's command to be introduced to Lord Wymondham.

"How do you do, Lady Jane?" he said in a deep voice. Jane held out her hand to be shaken and looked up into David's eyes.

A shock ran through her whole body. She heard herself mechanically replying to his words. She could not drag her eyes from his face.

He looks like David. He looks like David. The refrain ran insistently through her brain. When Mrs. Andrews arrived, she had just enough presence of mind left to say, "I'll show Lord Wymondham to his room, Uncle Edward. The blue room, Mrs. Andrews?"

"Yes, Lady Jane."

"Come this way, Lord Wymondham." She turned and led the way up the great staircase. All the way she was thinking furiously. This resemblance could not be an accident. It had to have something to do with Wrexham's behavior. By the time they reached the Blue Room she had made up her mind.

She held the door for the Earl to enter, then came in herself and closed the door behind her. He turned to look at her, surprise turning his eyes golden. Jane swallowed, then said determinedly, "My lord, I must ask you a question."

The slightly wary expression on his face was achingly familiar. "Must it be asked behind closed doors, Lady Jane?"

"Yes. I want to ask you if you ever knew a girl named Jeanne Dumont."

The Earl looked like a man who had suddenly been hit over the head. "Why do you ask me this?" he said finally, his voice harsh.

"Because her son has your eyes," said Jane.

Chapter XXII

My father!—methinks I see my father.
—William Shakespeare

He stared at her and the silence between them was fraught with emotion. Then, controlling visibly all his dazed senses, he said quietly, "Jeanne Dumont is dead. What do you know about her son?"

Jane's voice sounded slightly breathless, but otherwise it was as calm as his. "I know that his aunt took him out of France shortly after his mother died. She brought him here to Newmarket. He has lived here for seventeen years now."

The Earl, if possible, went even whiter than before. "He is here in Newmarket?"

"Yes."

Lord Wymondham was holding onto the back of a chair. His knuckles were white. "His aunt. What was her name?"

"Héloise Dumont. David's name is not Dumont. It is Chance. His father was the steward of a great estate in Artois. He was killed in the revolution." Jane looked at the Earl levelly, a challenge in her blue-green gaze. "But if Raoul La Chance was

179

David's father," she said, "Why does he look like you?"

"If this David is who he appears to be," the Earl said evenly, "Raoul La Chance is not his father. I am. I must see him. Where can I find him?"

"You will be rather a shock to him," Jane said grimly. "There has never even been a hint that he was a bastard."

"A bastard?" Lord Wymondham laughed. "If he is my son, Lady Jane, he is no bastard. I was married to Jeanne Dumont."

Jane's eyes began to blaze with excitement. "So that is it!" she said cryptically. "Of course." Her face took on an abstracted look. "I'll take you to David's cottage, Lord Wymondham. First, I must write a note to my uncle." She walked swiftly to a small secretary and, opening it, took out paper. She seated herself and wrote a few lines. Then she rose again. "I think it best if we go out the side door, my lord," she said. "We can explain matters to my uncle after you have met David."

Lord Wymondham agreed and followed her down the back staircase and out the door. They went down to the stables, where Jane ordered the phaeton and gave her note to be delivered to Lord Rayleigh. She took the reins and in a very short time they were pulling up before David's cottage.

As they drove, Jane had given the Earl a brief summary of David's position at Heathfield so that the modest, timber-framed house with its thatched roof was not a surprise to him. In actuality the immaculate white-plastered cottage set off the high-hedged lane looked comfortable and welcoming in the twilight. Jane glanced at the Earl. His face wore a look of tense, abstract steadfastness. "I'll go in first," she said.

Lord Wymondham nodded and allowed Jane to open the door. Inside, the room was worn and comfortable, a combination sitting room-dining room-kitchen. A tall man was bending over something in the oven. He turned at the sound of the opening door. "Jane!" he said, surprise and warmth in his deep, gentle voice. "I didn't expect to see you."

"Something very important has happened, David." She walked into the room and he saw for the first time the man in the doorway. He raised his brows in surprise.

"This is Lord Wymondham, David," she said in the quiet, toneless voice of deep intimacy. "I brought him to see you because he was married nineteen years ago to Jeanne Dumont."

There was a puzzled silence. "But Jeanne Dumont was my mother," David said blankly.

"I know," she replied steadily.

Bewildered, David turned from her to look at the man who had entered after her and for the first time Lord Wymondham faced his son. That David was his son there was no doubt. Looking at him, Lord Wymondham understood Jane's instant recognition. David's face was his own, purified and refined by the strange alchemy of biology into a beauty the Earl's harsher features had never possessed. But the resemblance was remarkable. The only thing of his mother about David was the color of his hair. For a moment it seemed impossible to the Earl. He had looked for the boy for so long. He had resigned himself to the loss. And now, to be confronted by this tall, strong, golden youngster who looked at him out of troubled eyes and said, "I don't understand."

"It is very simple, David," Jane said gently. "Lord Wymondham is your father."

David fixed his eyes on her. "Explain it to me," he said tensely.

She went to stand beside him, her head tipped back, her beautiful aquamarine eyes fixed steadily on his. As he watched them, the Earl realized that there was something between the boy and girl that went beyond friendship. "Don't you see, David," Jane concluded, "you are Lord Wymondham's true heir. His son. His only legitimate son."

David looked now at the Earl, his young face surprisingly grim. "Is there any proof of this?" he asked Lord Wymondham.

"The proof that you are my son lies in your own face, David," the Earl said gently. "As for the rest—it is no secret I was married in France. The marriage was registered. I went back to England to try to win over my family. Your mother was of good but not noble birth, and they were angry that I had married her. The Bastille had been stormed and many aristocrats were leaving France, but I never thought I would be unable to return. I should have brought her with me, of course, but

I was unsure of the reception that would await her. I wanted to smooth things down first myself. Then the royal family tried to escape and were captured at Varenes and brought back to Paris. The ports were closed and I couldn't get back. I was frantic. It wasn't until the following year that I persuaded an American passport out of the United States embassy and returned to France. I found that your mother was dead and that you, whose existence I had discovered for the first time, had been spirited out of Artois by your aunt."

"But why didn't Mlle. Dumont bring David to you?" asked Jane, who stood close beside David as if to give him support.

"She didn't know about me. Evidently Jeanne thought it was dangerous to let it be known that David's father, and her husband, was an English noble. It was a poor climate for aristocrats. She let everyone think the child was illegitimate. She refused to name the father."

"Even to her sister?"

"Héloise had been in Paris. She arrived in Artois after Jeanne had died. Evidently she invented this Raoul La Chance to save David the embarrassment of illegitimacy." He looked at his son. "I have never forgiven myself for leaving your mother. And I looked for you, David. In seventeen-ninety-two and again in eighteen-oh-two, when the Treaty of Amiens allowed the English to briefly return to France. There was no trace."

"I see." David's face was reserved. He obviously was not sure how to take this father suddenly resurrected from the void. A thought struck him as he looked at Lord Wymondham's authoritative face. "Jane!" he said excitedly. "Do you realize what this means about Wrexham?"

She nodded solemnly. "I do. Of course he saw the resemblance between you and Lord Wymondham immediately. And I remember how I took him up Marren Hill and let him pump me about your background. I very nicely provided him with all the necessary information to put two and two together."

"What is this about Julian?" Lord Wymondham asked imperatively.

Jane and David stared at him, the same speculative look in their eyes. Then Jane said, "I think we have to tell him, David."

David looked for another minute at his father, then he sighed. "I suppose so. At least now people won't think I'm crazy."

The Earl had borne their combined scrutiny with composure. Now he said, "Perhaps we could all sit down and then you can tell me about it. It has to do with Julian's death, I gather."

He had struck the chord of David's inborn courtesy. "I beg your pardon, sir, for keeping you standing. Please do sit down."

Jane sniffed. "Is that lamb stew in the oven, David?" At his nod she smiled for the first time since she had come in. "Oh, good. Mrs. Copley makes excellent lamb stew and I'm starving. Sit down, my lord." She gestured to the large table positioned in front of the fire. "By the time we get back to Heathfield, dinner will be over. We may as well eat here." She looked suddenly anxious. "I hope there's enough?"

David laughed. "I don't believe anything could take away your appetite, Jane. Yes, there should be enough. Mrs. Copley cooked for lunch tomorrow as well."

"Excellent. I'll set the table and serve. You tell Lord Wymondham about Wrexham."

So, as Jane dished out the stew, with an ease that betokened long familiarity, David told his father about Wrexham's attempts on his life. "I couldn't understand why he would do such a thing," he concluded. "He did say he couldn't allow me to take what was his, but that didn't mean anything to me."

Jane looked up from the last of her stew. "He said that? You never told me."

His gaze was serene. "I must have forgotten."

She raised an eyebrow. "Really?" she said skeptically. Then she transferred her eyes to Lord Wymondham. "What do you think we should do, my lord?" she asked.

There was a slight frown between the Earl's brows. "Exactly what you have done," he answered slowly, his eyes on his son. "Nothing. We will say that my discovering you like this was just an accident. I had come to Newmarket to bring home Julian's body and by chance discovered you working in Rayleigh's stables. No one who sees you will question the relationship."

"Evidently not," said David. "Wrexham and Jane seem to have picked it up right away."

Jane snorted. "I'm sorry if you liked your nephew, Lord Wymondham, but for my part, I'm glad David pushed him into the quarry. He was a snake, first trying to steal David's inheritance and then trying to kill him. He deserved what he got."

"I never greatly cared for Julian, Lady Jane, and I perfectly agree with you." Jane looked at the Earl approvingly as he pronounced these words.

"I didn't push him into the quarry, Jane," David protested. "He fell."

"Well, you should have pushed him," Jane said stubbornly. "*I* would have."

David suddenly grinned. "And then left his body for the vultures."

"Certainly." She rose from the table and began collecting the dishes. "I told you the stew was good," she commented as she took Lord Wymondham's empty plate.

"It was. Very good." The Earl looked at his napkin for a minute and then said carefully, "I want you to come home with me tomorrow, David. You are my son. My heir. It should not be difficult to take care of the legal side of things. You belong at Wymondham. It will be yours some day."

Astonishingly, David said, "I don't know."

The Earl raised his eyes and looked directly at David. "Why not?" he asked.

In answer, David looked at Jane. "Of course

you must go," she said. "Don't you see it's the perfect solution?"

He looked intensely serious. Of course he knew what she meant. If he approached Lord Rayleigh as the future Earl of Wymondham, his suit would almost certainly be accepted. He and Jane could marry without any of the scandal that would inevitably attach itself to an elopement. But he thought again of Anne. "How will I know if you're all right?"

"I'll write. Don't worry. Of course you must go," she repeated.

As Lord Wymondham watched them, he felt his face stiffening. The meaning of David's question did not escape him. So things had gone as far as that, he thought grimly. He was not pleased. He did not want to relinquish his son as soon as he was discovered. He wanted to make up to David all the things he'd missed during his lost years. He did not want David to marry at eighteen years of age.

None of this appeared on his face as he listened to Jane promising to write. David then said he did not want to accompany Wrexham's body back to Wymondham. He would come after the burial. Next week. With that, Lord Wymondham had to be content. For the first time in his life the Earl helped with the dishes and then he and Jane drove back to Heathfield.

Chapter XXIII

> ... all my fortunes at thy feet I'll lay
> And follow thee my lord throughout the world.
> —William Shakespeare

Lord and Lady Rayleigh were in the drawing room when Lord Wymondham and Jane returned. Jane's face was brilliant as they came into the beautiful, tapestry-hung room. "Don't be cross, Uncle Edward and Anne," she said. "We apologize for slipping out on you, but the most wonderful thing has happened. Oh, Anne, have you met Lord Wymondham?" Anne was staring at the Earl, a startled expression on her face, and when he spoke to her her eyes instinctively went to Jane. Jane was regarding her with an expression that could only be called triumphant.

Good breeding came to Anne's rescue. She asked Lord Wymondham to be seated and offered him a glass of brandy, which he accepted. He sipped it, glanced at Jane, and said, "Well, Lady Jane, the story by rights belongs to you, I believe. Suppose you start."

Jane's eyes sparked green fire. "Take a good look at Lord Wymondham," she said dramatically. "Whom does he remind you of?"

188

The Marquis frowned. "You know, he does remind me of someone. I thought so all afternoon. I supposed it must have been Wrexham."

Jane turned to Anne. "And what do you see, Anne?"

Anne said slowly, "I see a man who looks remarkably like David Chance."

Jane's smile was beatific. "With good reason, Anne. Lord Wymondham is David's father."

Lord Wymondham left Heathfield the next day, taking home with him the body of Julian Wrexham. Jane had told the Rayleighs the whole story of Wrexham's death and the Marquis had agreed with Lord Wymondham that the original explanation should not be tampered with. "An inquest was held," Lord Rayleigh had said. "If there is any talk, it will soon die down. Leave the dead man in peace."

Jane felt no compassion at all for the reputation of the dead Wrexham, but she did not want to make possible difficulties for David. Julian Wrexham's body was sent home with an outward show of regret by the whole Rayleigh family.

Scarcely anyone thought about him, however, once the coach was out of the drive. All anyone could talk about was David. The house and stable buzzed with comment. There was some awkwardness at first as people stumbled over how to address him. Properly speaking, as the heir to Wymondham he was now Lord Audley. When Stubbs called him that, however, David had first

looked startled and then had laughed. "Please
don't complicate my life any more than it is at
present," he had begged in his deep, gentle voice.
"Mr. David will do just fine, Stubbs."

He was the same. In the face of his extraordinary new fate, David remained David: courteous,
kind, thorough, and endlessly patient. He spent a
few days working in the stable. Anne had protested that it wasn't necessary, but David said it was.
Jane and Lord Rayleigh agreed. They followed
him about slavishly for two days, taking endless
mental and written notes on his soft-spoken comments on each horse and its progress. Jane and the
Marquis would have to run the stable until they
could hire another head trainer.

There wasn't a soul at Heathfield who wasn't
delighted for David and who wouldn't genuinely
miss him. Lord and Lady Rayleigh were perhaps
the happiest of all. "Have you seen the expression
on Jane's face when she looks at him?" Lord Rayleigh asked his wife one evening as they were talking in her bedroom.

Anne's eyes glinted with amusement. "She looks
positively smug," she asserted. "Like a vindicated
mama whose ugly duckling has miraculously
turned into a swan."

"Smug," he repeated. "That's it." He heaved a
sigh. "You've no idea what a weight has rolled off
my chest, Anne," he said. "Now if she wants to
marry him I can give my blessings in all good conscience. I simply could not have allowed her to

marry him before. And God knows what she would have done then, or forced me to do."

Anne, who remembered vividly Jane's elaborately casual questions about having babies, agreed fervently. She had been terrified when Jane, who had evinced no interest in her pregnancy thus far, had suddenly become inquisitive. She had been afraid to tell the Marquis of her suspicions. If Jane were having David Chance's child, God alone knew what he would do. Anne didn't, but the very thought petrified her.

Now, of course, everything was different. They could be married without committing any social sins. It would be an alliance between two of the oldest and noblest families in the country. Anne knew that Jane would have been ready to marry David if he had been a chimney sweep. If it had come to a confrontation over the question of marriage, Anne had unwillingly come to the conclusion that she would have to support Jane. The ordinary social conventions just didn't hold in this case. Several months of Jane's company had been very liberating for Anne. However, she could not but share the Marquis's relief. No one could have any objections to the marriage now.

Jane felt the same way. The day after Lord Wymondham had left, she had told David that everything was all right, she was not going to have a baby. There was no great pressure on them now. They could simply get engaged and then married like everybody else.

It was a plan that David wholeheartedly en-

dorsed. The night before he was due to leave for
Wymondham, Jane talked a footman into leaving
the side door open after everyone had gone to bed
and at two in the morning she sneaked out. She
went down the drive to the stables and slipped,
unobserved, into the tack room. There was a light
burning and David was waiting for her.

He bolted the door and turning, took her into
his arms for the first time since the night of Julian
Wrexham's death. She lifted her face to him and
their kiss had the intensity of lovers on the edge
of the void. Her slender body was arched up
against his. Her hands slid under his jacket to
hold him closer. He felt passion and surrender in
her mouth and looked with longing at the stack of
blankets on the floor. But then the thought of
Anne stabbed across his fevered brain and, with
taut lips and shaking hands, he put her away from
him.

"We can't, Jane," he grated. "We can't take the
chance."

She was trembling. "I don't care," she whispered.

"Well, I do," he said brutally. "We were lucky
before. We may not be again. I want to be able to
ask for you honorably and marry you honorably. I
don't want to have to face Lord Rayleigh, who has
never been anything but kind to me, and tell him
I've gotten his niece with child."

She looked at his tense mouth and pinched nostrils. She sighed. "You can't help being honorable,
I guess. It must be in your blood, or something."

At the mournful note in her voice his mouth relaxed. "I'm sorry, love," he said. "But it's for the best, believe me."

"Oh, I do," she responded glumly. "Uncle Edward is honorable, too. That's why he wouldn't have let me marry you before."

His lips twitched. "Men are terrible," he said gravely. "But you'll only have to put up with it for a short time. I'll explain how we feel to Lord Wymondham, and make the proper request to your uncle for your hand. I can't see anything that would stand in our way. If Lord Rayleigh was ready to accept one Wrexham for you, I expect he'll be willing to take another."

"Of course he will. And your father can hardly object to me."

David grinned at the complacency in her voice. "Of course not," he agreed.

She made a face at him. "Half of London wanted to marry me, I'll have you know. Lord Wymondham should know his son is getting a prize."

"*I* know I am," he said soberly. He held her face between his hands. "Jane."

In the dimly-lit room her eyes glowed like huge light gems. She smiled at him. Lightly she touched his cheek. "Check out Wymondham's stables, David. If we're going to live there, we may have a lot of rebuilding to do."

He laughed and bent to kiss the top of her head. "God got lucky on the day he made you," he told her. "Don't come to see me off tomorrow. I'll write as soon as possible."

"Yes sir," she said, mockingly sketching a curtsy.

"It won't be so bad, Jane. We've been separated before." He sounded as if he were reassuring himself.

She smiled a little wryly. "Let's hope this is the last time."

"It will be," he said intensely. "I couldn't go through this again."

It was worse for him, she knew. He was going to a strange place, to a position he had not been reared for, to a father he did not know. It would have been so much easier for him if she were there. "I know, David," she said softly. "It will be all right. Just be yourself. Everything will work out just fine. I know it will."

He reached out once more and pulled her against him. This time it was Jane who stepped back first. "I've got to get back," she said breathlessly.

"Yes." His face was still in the lamplight. "I won't say goodbye."

"No. I'll hear from you soon. Good luck, my love." She unbolted the door and went out. He watched as she went up the drive, her back very straight. She did not look around again.

Chapter XXIV

A plague o' both your houses!
—William Shakespeare

David came to Wymondham, principle seat of the Earls of Wymondham and his future home, on a clear day in early June. Lord Rayleigh had insisted upon sending him in his own coach so David at least had the comfort of traveling with familiar faces. They had made an early start and it was dinnertime by the time they reached Derbyshire.

As they entered the Earl's grounds, David sat forward in his seat, curious to see the land that was his heritage. The coach drove for some time through a beautiful wood which stretched on either side for as far as the eye could see. Gradually the ground rose and eventually the coach came out on the top of a hill which led down into a lovely valley. On the other side of the valley, backed by a ridge and high, woody hills and fronted by a stream, stood Wymondham House. David swallowed as he took in the magnificent stone building set so perfectly in the beautiful landscape. His forehead and the palms of his hands felt damp. How could he ever hope to live up to all this?

They descended the hill, crossed the bridge, and drove to the door. A major domo in magnificent livery came down the steps as Lord Rayleigh's footman sprang to open the coach door for David. As he descended, Tom, the redheaded footman he had known for years, winked at him. Some of the constriction left his throat and he winked back. Then, gravely, he walked up the stairs and into his father's house.

Lord Wymondham stood in the drawing room window and watched his son walking toward the house. David was dressed in buckskins and an old coat. He had been out riding again, the Earl realized. He watched the tall figure with its easy and unhurried stride until it passed out of his view in the shadow of the house.

The Earl was profoundly grateful for David. When he thought of what the boy could have been, given his upbringing, he realized how fortunate he had been. He remembered his nervousness on the first night of David's arrival as they had sat down to dinner. He had eaten with David once before, but the circumstances had been far removed from the elegant dining room at Wymondham with its priceless silver plate and china and its rows of hovering servants.

David's table manners had been faultless. Tante Héloise had had her foibles, but she had insisted that her nephew learn the manners of a gentleman. David's speech, also, was free of any lower-class accent or dialect. For that, if Lord

Wymondham had cared to inquire, he could thank Jane. David had spent his boyhood with her and not with the children of the townspeople; his speech reflected his company.

Actually, Lord Wymondham thought as he turned away from the window, there was very little to keep David from taking his place comfortably in the ranks of his peers. His clothing was atrocious, of course, but that was a problem easily remedied. The Earl had taken him into town to make some initial purchases; the rest of his wardrobe could be purchased from Weston once they went up to London.

In fact, there were only four areas where the Earl felt David needed tutoring. He didn't fence; he was a terrible shot; he rode magnificently but was a poor driver, and he didn't dance. The Earl had begun to teach him how to drive. David enjoyed that and he was a quick pupil. The Earl found great pleasure in it as well. There was little constriction between them as they drove behind his spirited grays, both intent on the same purpose. It was at these times he felt closest to his son.

The Earl had had less success in his endeavors to teach David to fence and to shoot. "I fail to see the point of it, sir," he had said in his quiet, courteous voice. "I have no intention of ever dueling with anyone, either with swords or with guns."

"Fencing is perhaps not necessary," Lord Wymondham agreed. "But you must learn to shoot. Every gentleman shoots, David."

"I know." A shade of distaste crossed David's face. "They kill birds and animals. I won't do it." He got his love of animals from his mother, the Earl thought. He remembered vividly how she would care for strays and injured wild things. But David was a man. He should learn to shoot.

"I am sorry, sir," David said finally, "I would like to oblige you. But I have no interest in shooting. None." And there the matter rested. Under the soft-spoken exterior, the Earl was discovering, David could be solid steel.

He had better luck with the dancing. David's initial impulse had been to refuse, but then he remembered that Jane danced. She might like to be able to dance with him. He acquiesced and a dancing master was engaged.

Three weeks after David's arrival at Wymondham, the Earl invited a few of his neighbors for a dinner party. It was David's first introduction into upper class society and it went very well. Sir Hubert and Lady Spenser had brought their eighteen-year-old daughter Clarissa, and it was obvious from the time that she first saw David that he was going to be a success with the girls. It was easy to see why, the Earl thought as he watched his son bend his head to listen to something Lady Mary Lorring was saying to him. He wore impeccable evening dress. His hair was freshly cut and neatly brushed across his forehead. He looked so new, Lord Wymondham thought, so pure and male and beautiful. There wasn't a woman in

London who wouldn't count herself lucky to stand talking to him.

He had gotten along very well with the men, also. "Damn fine boy, Wymondham," Sir Henry Mellon had grunted as they left the dining room to rejoin the ladies. "Extraordinary, your finding him like that."

After the company had gone, Lord Wymondham and David sat alone in the drawing room. The Earl had a glass of brandy in his hand. David had refused one. "I'm not used to drinking very much," he had said. "Tante Héloise never had anything in the house. In fact, the only time I ever had more than ale before coming here was when I was fourteen and Jane stole a couple of bottles of burgundy from her uncle's cellar."

Lord Wymondham raised his eyebrow encouragingly. David very rarely volunteered information about his past life. He was easy-going and courteous, but reticent. The Earl felt comfortable with him, but had no feeling of knowing him. If he had any inclination for confidences, the Earl would be most receptive. "What happened?" he asked.

David laughed. "We each drank a bottle. Jane got sick and threw up most of what she had drunk. I wasn't so lucky. I developed a splitting headache and felt miserable for the whole rest of the day. We never did it again."

The Earl smiled reminiscently. "I remember my brother and I doing exactly the same thing.

You'll learn to drink and to enjoy good wine, David. It takes time."

David smiled faintly. "If you say so, sir."

He had never yet called Lord Wymondham father. The Earl looked at him as he sat easily in the winged chair on the other side of the fire. He looked as at home in the high-ceilinged, silk-hung drawing room as he had in the shabby parlor of his cottage in Newmarket. There was a quality of relaxation about David, the Earl realized, that made him fit in wherever he happened to be. "I thought perhaps we would go up to London," he said into the silence. "You're still a bit young for the social scene, most young men your age are at Oxford or Cambridge, but a little town bronze wouldn't hurt you at all. Then we might do a little traveling. See the parts of the world Napoleon has left untrammeled so far."

David turned his eyes from their contemplation of the fire until they rested on his father's face. "You are very kind, sir," he said peacefully, "but there is really only one thing I want to do at the moment and that is to get married."

There was a deep line between the Earl's brows. "To Lady Jane Fitzmaurice, I take it."

"To Jane, yes."

"She's a beautiful girl," the Earl said objectively. "Good family, too. If you are of the same mind in a few years time and she's still available, I shouldn't object at all."

David sat up straight in his chair. "A few years' time!" he said sharply.

"Yes." The Earl was firm. "You are only eighteen years of age, David. You have seen nothing of the world. You are far too young to be tying yourself down in marriage. I want you to have the opportunities you missed all through your youth. It is very painful for me to think of my son working as a common groom. I can't tell you how I blame myself for your unfortunate childhood. But that is all finished with now. You are David Wrexham, Viscount Audley, and I want you to have a chance to enjoy your new position and your new freedom."

David's face was set and stern. He had been attending carefully to what his father was saying. "There is no need for you to feel pain because of what happened in the past," he answered now. "No blame attaches to you. You tried to find me. I certainly don't hold your failure against you." David's eyes dropped and he regarded his own strong, slender hand as it lay on the arm of his chair. "It was not, as you seem to think, an unhappy childhood. True, I had to work. But I loved what I was doing. I was very good at it. And," there was a pause, then he said softly, "there was Jane."

He looked up then and a golden light glowed deep in his eyes. "I was happy to discover that I was the son of an earl. Not because I wanted to leave my position or Heathfield, but because it meant I could marry Jane. I love her, father. I have never loved anyone else."

It was the first time David had ever addressed

him as father. The Earl clenched his hands into fists on his knees, stared at David a minute, then rose. "You have never known anyone else," he said definitely. "You are too young to marry. You are still a boy, David. Wait a while. You will be grateful to me in the future for this."

David looked up at his father thoughtfully, almost remotely. "And if I refuse?"

"You are a minor and my son. You cannot marry without my consent. We won't speak of this again, David," the Earl said with the authority of a man who is used to being obeyed. "My decision is final."

Chapter XXV

It is my soul that calls upon my name. . . .
—William Shakespeare

David awoke early the next morning after a troubled night's sleep. As he lay, arms behind his head, watching the sun slanting through the blinds the door opened and one of the maids came in. "Oh, I beg your pardon, my lord," she said. "I didn't know you were still here."

It was six-thirty in the morning. David looked at her without speaking and she came and stood at the foot of the bed. Her eyes sparkled and she thrust her hips forward. "Is there anything I can do for you?" she asked demurely, her dark eyes fixed appreciatively on the man lying so watchfully before her.

A flicker passed across David's face, then all expression was shuttered off. "No," he replied evenly. "There is nothing you can do for me."

After she had gone, he rose and went to the window. From his bedroom he could see the river, the trees scattered on its bank, and the lovely, winding valley. The view was beautiful but it appeared to offer no solace to its future owner. The expression on David's face was bleak.

The conversation with his father last night had stunned him. The Earl's denial had been so unexpected that David had found no words to argue with him. It had never occurred to him that Lord Wymondham would object. He was accustomed to regarding Lord Rayleigh as his stumbling block, accustomed to thinking himself not good enough for Jane. He had been stunned to find that his father thought *he* was too young to marry. He had been in sole charge of his own life since he was sixteen; he had worked for a living since before that. It was astounding to find that Lord Wymondham apparently thought he could dictate the course of his life for him.

He had been too angry and too stunned to say much to his father last night and as he lay sleepless he had realized the wisdom of that approach. There really was nothing else he could say. There was only one solution to the problem, the solution he had arrived at before Lord Wymondham entered the picture: He and Jane would have to elope.

Lord Wymondham would doubtless be very angry. Perhaps, David thought, he would refuse to recognize him as his son. David didn't care. He only knew that he had to marry Jane.

Throughout the weeks of his sojourn at Wymondham, he had tried not to think about her. He had forced himself to wait until he felt confident that his new role in life was going to be workable. Last night's party had been a test, and he knew he had passed it. That was why he had spoken to his father about marrying Jane.

The Earl's refusal had unleashed the floodgates of his longing, and the haunting feeling of incompleteness, of irreparable loss that always ran below the surface of his life when he was separated from Jane, broke through its restraints. The ache of her absence was like an open wound. It had always been painful; now it was intolerable. The night they had spent together made this separation so much worse than any other. He needed her. For a brief moment he had thought to use the maid to assuage some of his aching hunger, but almost instantly he knew the futility of even trying. It was Jane he wanted. With an intensity of purpose that sprang from desperation, David began to make his plans.

With some reluctance Lord Wymondham agreed to a stop at Newmarket on their way to London. "I must see Jane," David had said firmly. "She expects me to make an offer for her. I must explain things to her."

The Earl had reason to believe that Jane was owed an explanation and so he acquiesced in David's desire. Messages were sent to Heathfield and Lord Wymondham and his son were graciously invited to make a stay with the Marquis and Marchioness of Rayleigh. The Earl agreed to one night. He did not want to expose David to Jane's influence for too long a period.

He was pleased that David was behaving sensibly. Obviously he had considered what the Earl had said and had decided it was reasonable. At eighteen, he was much too young to tie himself down.

In fact, David had been emulating Jane's strategy when she found herself expected to marry Julian Wrexham. He said little and seemed to accept the Earl's decision. Unlike the Marquis, who had been alarmed by Jane's uncharacteristic docility, the Earl was gratified. He did not know David well enough to take fright.

The Earl sent two coaches ahead of them to London, heaped with luggage and servants. He and David took the phaeton and a few bags and drove by themselves to Newmarket. It was a warm, sunny day and Lord Wymondham was delighted with David's driving prowess. David made a great effort to overcome his preoccupation and was more talkative than he had been in weeks. Consequently, the Earl was in good spirits as they pulled into the Heathfield drive.

David felt as if he were coming home. Lord and Lady Rayleigh received them in the drawing room. Jane was not there. Correctly interpreting the look on his face, Anne said, "Jane hasn't come back yet from her ride. I'm sure she—" She was interrupted by the sound of a door opening.

"David!" Jane cried, joy and some other emotion trembling in the clear cadences of her voice.

David spun around as if he had been shot. He had prepared his face to greet her earlier, but her sudden appearance now undid him. For a long moment he stood looking at her and his father had a clear view of his unguarded face. What he saw there caused the breath to catch for a moment in his throat.

Taken by surprise, David's expression was painfully revealing. He looked at Jane and his face was the face of a man, not a boy, full of a naked, speechless hunger that caused his father to avert his eyes. No one should see so clearly into another man's soul. Lord Wymondham turned his eyes to Jane and what he saw there gave him little comfort. She stood silent, looking at David as if there were no one else who existed in the room, as if there were no one else who existed in the world. With a profound pang the Earl remembered that once, nineteen years ago, a girl had looked like that at him.

He turned back to look at her son. David slowly began to walk across the room to where Jane stood at the door. "I have to talk to you, Jane," he said, his voice slightly unsteady. "Let's go to the library."

Without a word she turned and led him out of the room. The door closed behind them, leaving the Rayleighs and Lord Wymondham alone together. No one made any attempt to follow them. The Marquis turned to face David's father. "What happened?" he asked. "I was afraid there was something wrong when you said you would only stay one night."

The Earl did not pretend to misunderstand. "I told him I did not want him to marry for a few years."

"Oh, my God." Lord Rayleigh walked to the window and back. "I don't think you quite understand the situation, Wymondham," he said finally.

"Perhaps you had better tell me, Rayleigh," the Earl said slowly. "I think perhaps I do not."

In the library, David was standing with Jane's hands clasped tightly in his own, his eyes devouring her face. "We shall have to elope," he said.

"I knew something was wrong." Her voice was surprisingly serene. "All right, we'll elope. Don't look so worried. Shall we go tonight?"

His face lightened and once again he looked his age. "There's no one like you, Jane. Yes. Tonight. I'll meet you at the side door at two o'clock."

Her great blue-green eyes began to sparkle. "Are we going to Scotland?"

"We'll have to." There was a pause, then he said, "He doesn't think I should get married for a few years. He may cut me off, Jane, if we do this."

She shrugged. "We don't need Wymondham. We can manage by ourselves. You aren't some ridiculous dandy who never learned how to do a day's work."

He smiled. Now that he was with her, things suddenly seemed so much easier. He smoothed her hair off her forehead. "And you aren't a drawing-room lady afraid to soil her hands on a parvenue like myself." His mouth took on an obstinate look. "I don't want Wymondham if I can't have you. The price is too high. If you're not there the most beautiful place in the world might as well be a desert as far as I'm concerned."

"Why does your father want you to wait, David?" she asked curiously.

"He says I'm too young." He looked down into her beautiful face and his eyes narrowed. "Perhaps he's right. Perhaps we're both too young for what we feel. But that doesn't alter the fact that we feel it. He's a nice man, Jane, but he doesn't understand. He couldn't. He doesn't know us."

She was standing close to him, her head tipped back to look up into his face. His fingers moved caressingly along the fine line of her jaw to the back of her head. "It's been hell without you," he said low.

She stood perfectly still. Her eyes had darkened. "I know," she whispered.

He bent his head and began to kiss her.

Lord Rayleigh did know Jane and David, and he was attempting to explain the situation to Lord Wymondham. "I can't tell you how relieved I was when David turned out to be your son," he said frankly. "You understand that I could hardly have allowed Jane to marry him before, but I tell you honestly I lived in daily dread of having a confrontation with her about it." He smiled wryly. "I hope I don't sound cowardly, my lord, but I would rather face a troop of Napoleon's best dragoons, single-handed, than have to face Jane and tell her she can't marry David."

"I rather thought she was going to marry my nephew," Lord Wymondham said stiffly.

"I had hopes at first," the Marquis said wearily. "But once we got back to Heathfield, I knew it was no good."

"Jane refused him, you know," Anne said in her gentle voice. "She said she needed time to think about it. What she needed, I think, was time to talk to David." Anne smoothed her skirt, avoiding the eyes of both men. "I always wondered why she showed a preference for Mr. Wrexham. Now I know. Facially he somewhat resembled David." She ran her fingers carefully over the figured muslin of her skirt. "I thought she and David were going to elope."

"What!" The Marquis stared at her in horror. "You never said anything about that to me."

"I know." She still refused to meet his eyes. "I was rather in sympathy with them, I'm afraid. Besides, what could you have done about it, Edward? What *would* you have done?" She raised her eyes now and fixed a gentle blue gaze on Lord Wymondham. "Those two children love each other, my lord. They love each other quite intensely, as a matter of fact. If we refuse to allow them to marry with our blessing, they will marry without it. Or they will simply go away and live together. They will both be ruined socially and it will have been our fault."

The Marquis looked at his wife, respect in his eyes. "What do you think he is saying to her now?" he asked.

"Whatever it is," Anne replied matter-of-factly, "you can be sure it isn't goodbye."

"He is only eighteen years old," the Earl said abruptly.

"And Jane is seventeen. But this is not a case of youthful infatuation we are dealing with, Lord Wymondham." Anne was pitiless. "They have loved each other exclusively for eleven years. I am sure David will grow quite fond of you, but the only person he will ever really love is Jane."

"Oh, I say, Anne," the Marquis expostulated, seeing a shadow cross Lord Wymondham's face.

"It is true," Anne said inexorably. "It is the same with Jane. She is very attached to you, Edward, but. . . ." She let the sentence dangle.

"I know." He sighed. "I remember once I asked her if she ever thought of anyone except David. She said of course she did. She thought about me and her drawing teacher and the horses. I'm afraid that's about where I rank. And if she thought it would save David the slightest discomfort, she would unhesitatingly throw me, Miss Becker, the horses, and you, too, Anne, over the nearest cliff. Anne is right about David, Wymondham. He feels the same way about Jane. I've known that for a long time." He hesitated. "I don't know if you've ever seen his face when he looks at her."

"I did just now," the Earl said harshly.

"Yes. Well, then you know what I mean."

As they were speaking the door opened and Jane and David came in. Their faces were identically expressionless. The Earl looked at them for a moment in silence, then he said, "Has David told you my decision, Lady Jane?"

"Yes," she answered composedly. "We don't agree with you, Lord Wymondham, but I suppose there is nothing we can do about it."

"You could always elope," he said bluntly.

The way their eyes flew together in startled consternation was evidence enough. Instinctively, David's hand went up to rest possessively on the nape of Jane's neck. He said nothing, only stared at his father out of hostile, golden eyes.

The Earl looked at that hand, and at both of their faces. He sighed. He knew when he was beaten; he was not a diplomat for nothing. "I have been talking to Lord and Lady Rayleigh," he said to his son. "It seems I have made a mistake. There will be no need for you to elope. You may be married here at Heathfield in a proper ceremony. I will be happy to attend. Afterward you may live at Wymondham."

There was a flash of color as Jane raised her eyes to David. He was looking straight at his father, equal to equal. "You are quite sure of that, sir?"

"Yes. You have my word on it."

"When?"

The Earl shrugged. "That will be up to the ladies."

They all stared at Anne. "A month," she said crisply. "If we wait any longer than that, I won't be fit to do much of anything."

Jane smiled brilliantly. "You are a Trojan, Anne." Uncharacteristically, she walked over to Anne and kissed her on the cheek.

"Congratulations, David!" the Marquis said heartily. "Lady Rayleigh and I have been sobbing noisily on your father's shoulder, begging him to let you take Jane off our hands. He has taken pity on our desperation."

David laughed, his eyes bright with unspoken feelings. "It's perfectly true," Jane said happily. "I would have made your life a hell on earth, Uncle Edward. David is the only one who could stand a lifetime of me."

David looked at her and there was a little steady flame deep in the amber of his eyes. Then he turned to Lord Wymondham. "Thank you, father," he said, and for the first time smiled at the Earl with unshadowed happiness.

The Earl clasped him briefly on the shoulder. "I only wanted what was best for you, my son."

"I know that. But, you see, what is best for me is Jane."

"I see it now," the Earl said dryly. He turned to where Jane was talking to her uncle. "Lord Rayleigh, perhaps you and I can discuss the question of marriage settlements."

Jane came across to stand beside David. "That's a good idea," she said cordially. "It will make David feel so much better not to have to live on my money."

She smiled at their suddenly stern faces, sublimely unconscious of having confirmed all of their darkest suspicions. The Earl recovered first. He said to David, who was regarding him with amused comprehension, "I'm sure you and Lady Jane have many things to say to each other while Lord Rayleigh and I discuss this matter."

Jane looked suddenly alert. "We certainly do, Lord Wymondham. Come along, David, I want you to look at Pericles. He has been quite sluggish the last few days."

David frowned. "He has? Has Hammond been to see him?" He walked to the door with Jane and then, remembering, turned back to the others. "Is it all right if I look at him, my lord?" he asked the Marquis.

Lord Rayleigh did not appear to be at all surprised by the turn the conversation was taking. "By all means, David. I should be grateful." Jane and David exited and they could hear her voice earnestly explaining to him the various symptoms she had noticed in the horse's behavior of late.

The Earl turned from the door, his mouth quivering slightly. His eyes met Anne's. "Are they really going to the stables?" he asked.

She laughed. "Of course. I told you they were perfectly suited to one another."

Lord Wymondham's autocratic features relaxed and he smiled back at her. "I see what you mean, Lady Rayleigh. I see what you mean."

About the Author

Joan Wolf is a native of New York City who presently resides in Milford, Connecticut, with her husband and two young children. She taught high school English in New York for nine years and took up writing when she retired to rear a family. Her previous books, THE COUNTERFEIT MARRIAGE and A KIND OF HONOR, are also available in Signet editions.

More Regency Romances from SIGNET

Buy them at your local
bookstore or use coupon
on next page for ordering.